A MOUNTAIN EUROPA

A CUMBERLAND VENDETTA

THE LAST STETSON

The scratch of the point on the hard steel.

A MOUNTAIN EUROPA

A CUMBERLAND VENDETTA

THE LAST STETSON

BY

JOHN FOX, JR.

ILLUSTRATED BY
F. C. YOHN AND LOUIS LOEB

NEW YORK
CHARLES SCRIBNER'S SONS
1914

CONTENTS

PAGE

A MOUNTAIN EUROPA 1

A CUMBERLAND VENDETTA . . . 115

THE LAST STETSON 233

ILLUSTRATIONS

"The scratch of the point on the hard steel". *Frontispiece*

FACING
PAGE

"'Why don't ye shoot?'" 142

"'We hain't fightin' women!'" 196

"Pray fer yer enemies, Eli" 262

A MOUNTAIN EUROPA

TO

JAMES LANE ALLEN

I

A S Clayton rose to his feet in the still air, the tree-tops began to tremble in the gap below him, and a rippling ran through the leaves up the mountain-side. Drawing off his hat he stretched out his arms to meet it, and his eyes closed as the cool wind struck his throat and face and lifted the hair from his forehead. About him the mountains lay like a tumultuous sea—the Jellico Spur, stilled gradually on every side into vague, purple shapes against the broken rim of the sky, and Pine Mountain and the Cumberland Range racing in like breakers from the north. Under him lay Jellico Valley, and just visible in a wooded cove, whence Indian Creek crept into sight, was a mining-camp—a cluster of white cabins—from which he had climbed that afternoon. At that distance the wagon-road narrowed to a bridle-path, and the figure moving slowly along it and entering the forest at the base of the mountain was shrunk to a toy. For a moment Clayton stood with his face to the west, drinking in the air; then tightening his belt, he caught the pliant body of a sapling and swung loose from the rock. As the tree flew back, his dog sprang after him. The descent was sharp. At times he was forced to cling to the birch-tops till they lay flat on the mountain-side.

Breathless, he reached at last a bowlder from which the path was easy to the valley below, and he leaned quivering against the soft rug of moss and lichens that covered it. The shadows had crept from the foot of the mountains, darkening the valley, and lifting up the mountain-side beneath him a long, wavering line in which met the cool, deep green of the shade and the shining bronze where the sunlight still lay. Lazily following this line, his eye caught two moving shadows that darted jagged shapes into the sunlight and as quickly withdrew them. As the road wound up toward him, two figures were soon visible through the undergrowth. Presently a head bonneted in blue rose above the bushes, and Clayton's half-shut eyes opened wide and were fixed with a look of amused expectancy where a turn of the path must bring rider and beast into plain sight. Apparently some mountain girl, wearied by the climb or in a spirit of fun, had mounted her cow while driving it home; and with a smile at the thought of the confusion he would cause her, Clayton stepped around the bowlder and waited. With

4

the slow, easy swing of climbing cattle, the beast brought its rider into view. A bag of meal lay across its shoulders, and behind this the girl—for she was plainly young—sat sidewise, with her bare feet dangling against its flank. Her face was turned toward the valley below, and her loosened bonnet half disclosed a head of bright yellow hair.

Catching sight of Clayton, the beast stopped and lifted its head, not the meek, patient face he expected to see, but a head that was wrinkled and vicious—the head of a bull. Only the sudden remembrance of a dead mountain custom saved him from utter amazement. He had heard that when beasts of burden were scarce, cows, and especially bulls, were worked in ploughs and ridden by the mountaineers, even by the women. But this had become a tradition, the humor of which greater prosperity and contact with a new civilization had taught even the mountain people to appreciate. The necessities of this girl were evidently as great as her fear of ridicule seemed small. When the brute stopped, she began striking him in the flank with her bare heel, without looking around, and as he paid no attention to such painless goading, she turned with sudden impatience and lifted a switch above his shoulders. The stick was arrested in mid-air when she saw Clayton, and then dropped harmlessly. The quick fire in her eyes died suddenly away, and for a moment the two looked at each other with mutual curiosity, but only for a moment. There was something in Clayton's gaze that displeased her. Her face clouded, and she dropped her eyes.

"G'long," she said, in a low tone. But the bull had lowered his head, and was standing with feet planted apart and tail waving uneasily. The girl looked up in alarm.

"Watch out thar!" she called out, sharply. "Call that dog off—quick!"

Clayton turned, but his dog sprang past him and began to bark. The bull, a lean, active, vicious-looking brute, answered with a snort.

"Call him off, I tell ye!" cried the girl, angrily, springing to the ground. "Git out o' the way. Don't you see he's a-comin' at ye?"

The dog leaped nimbly into the bushes, and the maddened bull was carried on by his own impetus toward Clayton, who, with a quick spring, landed in safety in a gully below the road. When he picked himself up from the uneven ground where he had fallen, the beast had disappeared around the bowlder. The bag had fallen, and had broken open, and some of the meal was spilled on the ground. The girl, flushed and angry, stood above it.

6

"Look thar, now," she said. "See whut you've done. Why'n't ye call that dog off?"

"I couldn't," said Clayton, politely. "He wouldn't come. I'm sorry, very sorry."

"Can't ye manage yer own dog?" she asked, half contemptuously.

"Not always."

"Then ye oughter leave him to home, and not let him go round a-skeerin' folks' beastes." With a little gesture of indignation she stooped and began scooping up the meal in her hand.

"Let me help you," said Clayton. The girl looked up in surprise.

"You go 'way," she said.

But Clayton stayed, watching her helplessly. He wanted to carry the bag for her, but she swung it to her shoulder, and moved away. He followed her around the bowlder, where his late enemy was browsing peacefully on sassafras-bushes.

"You stay thar now," said the girl, "and keep that dog back."

"Won't you let me help you get up?" he asked.

Without answering, the girl sprang lightly to the bull's back. Once only she looked around at him. He took off his hat, and a puzzled expression came into her face. Then, without a

7

word or a nod, she rode away. Clayton watched
the odd pair till the bushes hid them.

"Europa, by *Jove!*" he exclaimed, and he
sat down in bewilderment.

She was so very odd a creature, so different
from the timid mountain women who shrank
with averted faces almost into the bushes when
he met them. She had looked him straight in
the face with steady eyes, and had spoken as
though her sway over mountain and road were
undisputed and he had been a wretched tres-
passer. She paid no attention to his apologies,
and she scorned his offers of assistance. She
seemed no more angered by the loss of the meal
than by his incapacity to manage his dog,
which seemed to typify to her his general worth-
lessness. He had been bruised by his fall, and
she did not even ask if he were hurt. Indeed,
she seemed not to care, and she had ridden away
from him as though he were worth no more consideration than the stone under him.

He was amused, and a trifle irritated. How
could there be such a curious growth in the
mountains? he questioned, as he rose and continued the descent. There was an unusual
grace about her, in spite of her masculine air.
Her features were regular, the nose straight and
delicate, the mouth resolute, the brow broad,
and the eyes intensely blue, perhaps tender,

8

when not flashing with anger, and altogether without the listless expression he had marked in other mountain women, and which, he had noticed, deadened into pathetic hopelessness later in life. Her figure was erect, and her manner, despite its roughness, savored of something high-born. Where could she have got that bearing? She belonged to a race whose descent, he had heard, was unmixed English; upon whose lips lingered words and forms of speech that Shakespeare had heard and used. Who could tell what blood ran in her veins?

Musing, he had come almost unconsciously to a spur of the mountains under which lay the little mining-camp. It was six o'clock, and the miners, grim and black, each with a pail in hand and a little oil-lamp in his cap, were going down from work. A shower had passed over the mountains above him, and the last sunlight, coming through a gap in the west, struck the rising mist and turned it to gold. On a rock which thrust from the mountain its gray, sombre face, half embraced by a white arm of the mist, Clayton saw the figure of a woman. He waved his hat, but the figure stood motionless, and he turned into the woods toward the camp.

It was the girl; and when Clayton disappeared she too turned and went on her way. She had stopped there because she knew he must pass a point where she might see him again. She was little less indifferent than she seemed; her motive was little more than curiosity. She had never seen that manner of man before. Evidently he was a " furriner " from the " settlemints." No man in the mountains had a smooth, round face like his, or wore such a queer hat, such a soft, white shirt, and no " galluses," or carried such a shiny, weak-looking stick, or owned a dog that he couldn't make mind him. She was not wholly contemptuous, however. She had felt vaguely the meaning of his politeness and deference. She was puzzled and pleased, she scarcely knew why.

" He was mighty accomodatin'," she thought. " But whut," she asked herself as she rode slowly homeward—" whut did he take off his hat fer? "

II

LIGHTS twinkled from every cabin as
Clayton passed through the camp. Outside the kitchen doors, miners, bare to the waist,
were bathing their blackened faces and bodies,
with children, tattered and unclean, but health-
ful, playing about them; within, women in
loose gowns, with sleeves uprolled and with disordered hair, moved like phantoms through
clouds of savory smoke. The commissary was
brilliantly lighted. At a window close by im-
provident miners were drawing the wages of
the day, while their wives waited in the store
with baskets unfilled. In front of the commissary a crowd of negroes were talking, laughing, singing, and playing pranks like children.
Here two, with grinning faces, were squared off,
not to spar, but to knock at each other's tattered
hat; there two more, with legs and arms indis-
tinguishable, were wrestling; close by was the
sound of a mouth-harp, a circle of interested
spectators, and, within, two dancers pitted
against each other, and shuffling with a zest that
labor seemed never to affect.

Immediately after supper Clayton went to his room, lighted his lamp, and sat down to a map he was tracing. His room was next the ground, and a path ran near the open window. As he worked, every passer-by would look curiously within. On the wall above his head a pair of fencing-foils were crossed under masks. Below these hung two pistols, such as courteous Claude Duval used for side-arms. Opposite were two old rifles, and beneath them two stone beer-mugs, and a German student's pipe absurdly long and richly ornamented. A mantel close by was filled with curiosities, and near it hung a banjo unstrung, a tennis-racket, and a blazer of startling colors. Plainly they were relics of German student life, and the odd contrast they made with the rough wall and ceiling suggested a sharp change in the fortunes of the young worker beneath. Scarcely six months since he had been suddenly summoned home from Germany. The reason was vague, but having read of recent American failures, notably in Wall Street, he knew what had happened. Reaching New York, he was startled by the fear that his mother was dead, so gloomy was the house, so subdued his sister's greeting, and so worn and sad his father's face. The trouble, however, was what he had guessed, and he had accepted it with quiet resignation. The financial wreck seemed complete; but one resource, however, was left. Just after the war Clayton's father had purchased mineral lands in the South, and it was with the idea of developing these that he had encouraged the marked scientific tastes of his son, and had sent him to a German university. In view of his own disaster, and the fact that a financial tide was swelling southward, his forethought seemed an inspiration. To this resource Clayton turned eagerly; and after a few weeks at home, which were made intolerable by straitened circumstances, and the fancied coldness of friend and acquaintance, he was hard at work in the heart of the Kentucky mountains.

The transition from the careless life of a student was swift and bitter; it was like beginning a new life with a new identity, though Clayton suffered less than he anticipated. He had become interested from the first. There was nothing in the pretty glen, when he came, but a mountaineer's cabin and a few gnarled old apple-trees, the roots of which checked the musical flow of a little stream. Then the air was filled with the tense ring of hammer and saw, the mellow echoes of axes, and the shouts of ox-drivers from the forests, indignant groans from the mountains, and a little town sprang up before his eyes, and cars of shin-

ing coal wound slowly about the mountain-
side.

Activity like this stirred his blood. Busy
from dawn to dark, he had no time to grow miserable. His work was hard, to be sure, but it
made rest and sleep a luxury, and it had the new
zest of independence; he even began to take in
it no little pride when he found himself an es-
sential part of the quick growth going on.
When leisure came, he could take to woods
filled with unknown birds, new forms of insect
life, and strange plants and flowers. With
every day, too, he was more deeply stirred by
the changing beauty of the mountains—hidden
at dawn with white mists, faintly veiled through
the day with an atmosphere that made him think
of Italy, and enriched by sunsets of startling
beauty. But strongest of all was the interest
he found in the odd human mixture about him—
the simple, good-natured darkies who slouched
past him, magnificent in physique and picturesque with rags; occasional foreigners just from
Castle Garden, with the hope of the New
World still in their faces; and now and then a
gaunt mountaineer stalking awkwardly in the
rear of the march toward civilization. Gradually it had dawned upon him that this last, silent figure, traced through Virginia, was closely
linked by blood and speech with the common

people of England, and, moulded perhaps by the influences of feudalism, was still strikingly unchanged; that now it was the most distinctively national remnant on American soil, and symbolized the development of the continent, and that with it must go the last suggestions of the pioneers, with their hardy physiques, their speech, their manners and customs, their simple architecture and simple mode of life. It was soon plain to him, too, that a change was being wrought at last—the change of destruction. The older mountaineers, whose bewildered eyes watched the noisy signs of an unintelligible civilization, were passing away. Of the rest, some, sullen and restless, were selling their homesteads and following the spirit of their forefathers into a new wilderness; others, leaving their small farms in adjacent valleys to go to ruin, were gaping idly about the public works, caught up only too easily by the vicious current of the incoming tide. In a century the mountaineers must be swept away, and their ignorance of the tragic forces at work among them gave them an unconscious pathos that touched Clayton deeply.

As he grew to know them, their historical importance yielded to a genuine interest in the people themselves. They were densely ignorant, to be sure; but they were natural, simple, and hospitable. Their sense of personal worth was high, and their democracy—or aristocracy, since there was no distinction of caste—absolute. For generations, son had lived like father in an isolation hardly credible. No influence save such as shook the nation ever reached them. The Mexican war, slavery, and national politics of the first half-century were still present issues, and each old man would give his rigid, individual opinion sometimes with surprising humor and force. He went much among them, and the rugged old couples whom he found in the cabin porches—so much alike at first—quickly became distinct with a quaint individuality. Among young or old, however, he had found nothing like the half-wild young creature he had met on the mountain that day. In her a type had crossed his path—had driven him from it, in truth—that seemed unique and inexplicable. He had been little more than amused at first, but a keen interest had been growing in him with every thought of her. There was an indefinable charm about the girl. She gave a new and sudden zest to his interest in mountain life; and while he worked, the incidents of the encounter on the mountain came minutely back to him till he saw her again as she rode away, her supple figure swaying with every movement of the beast, and dappled with quivering circles of sunlight from the bushes, her face calm, but still flushed with color, and her yellow hair shaking about her shoulders—not lustreless and flaxen, as hair was in the mountains, he remembered, but catching the sunlight like gold.

Almost unconsciously he laid aside his pencil and leaned from his window to lift his eyes to the dark mountain he had climbed that day. The rude melody of an old-fashioned hymn was coming up the glen, and he recognized the thin, quavering voice of an old mountaineer, Uncle Tommy Brooks, as he was familiarly known, whose cabin stood in the midst of the camp, a pathetic contrast to the smart new houses that had sprung around it. The old man had lived in the glen for nearly three-quarters of a century, and he, if any one, must know the girl. With the thought, Clayton sprang through the window, and a few minutes later was at the cabin. The old man sat whittling in the porch, joining in the song with which his wife was crooning a child to sleep within. Clayton easily identified Europa, as he had christened her; the simple mention of her means of transport was sufficient.

"Ridin' a bull, was she?" repeated the old man, laughing. "Well, that was Easter Hicks, old Bill Hicks' gal. She's a sort o' connection o' mine. Me and Bill married cousins.

17

She's a cur'us critter as ever I seed. She don'
seem to take atter her dad nur her mammy
nother, though Bill allus had a quar streak in 'im,
and was the wust man I ever seed when he was
disguised by licker. Whar does she live? Oh,
up thar, right on top o' Wolf Mountain, with
her mammy."

"Alone?"

"Yes; fer her dad ain't thar. No; 'n' he
ain't dead. I'll tell ye"—the old man lowered
his tone—"thar used to be a big lot o' moon-
shinin' done in these parts, 'n' a raider come
hyeh to see 'bout it. Well, one mornin' he
was found layin' in the road with a bullet through
him. Bill was s'picioned. Now, I ain't a-sayin'
as Bill done it, but when a whole lot more rode
up thar on hosses one night, they didn't find Bill.
They hain't found him yit, fer he's out in the
mountains somewhar a-hidin'."

"How do they get along without him?"
asked Clayton.

"Why, the gal does the work. She ploughs
with that bull, and does the plantin' herself.
She kin chop wood like a man. An' as fer
shootin', well, when huntin's good 'n' thar's
shootin'-matches round-about, she don't have to
buy much meat."

"It's a wonder some young fellow hasn't married her. I suppose, though, she's too young."

18

A MOUNTAIN EUROPA

The old man laughed. " Thar's been many
a lively young fellow that's tried it, but she's
hard to ketch as a wildcat. She won't have
nothin' to do with other folks, 'n' she nuver
comes down hyeh into the valley, 'cept to git her
corn groun' er to shoot a turkey. Sherd Raines
goes up to see her, and folks say he air tryin' to
git her into the church. But the gal won't go
nigh a meetin'-house. She air a cur'us critter,"
he concluded emphatically, " shy as a deer till
she air stirred up, and then she air a caution;
mighty gentle sometimes, and ag'in stubborn as
a mule."

A shrill, infantile scream came from within,
and the old man paused a moment to listen.

" Ye didn't know I had a great-grandchild,
did ye? That's it a-hollerin'. Talk about
Easter bein' too young to merry! Why hit's
mother air two year younger'n Easter. Jes
come in hyeh a minit." The old mountaineer
rose and led the way into the cabin. Clayton
was embarrassed at first. On one bed lay a
rather comely young woman with a child by her
side; on a chest close by sat another with her
lover, courting in the most open and primitive
manner. In the corner an old grandam dozed
with her pipe, her withered face just touched by
the rim of the firelight. Near a rectangular
hole in the wall which served the purpose of a

19

window, stood a girl whose face, silhouetted against the darkness, had in it a curious mixture of childishness and maturity.

"Whar's the baby?" asked Uncle Tommy.

Somebody outside was admiring it, and the young girl leaned through the window and lifted the infant within.

"Thar's a baby fer ye!" exclaimed the old mountaineer, proudly, lifting it in the air and turning its face to the light. But the child was peevish and fretful, and he handed it back gently. Clayton was wondering which was the mother, when, to his amazement, almost to his confusion, the girl lifted the child calmly to her own breast. The child was the mother of the child. She was barely fifteen, with the face of a girl of twelve, and her motherly manner had struck him as an odd contrast. He felt a thrill of pity for the young mother as he called to mind the aged young wives he had seen who were haggard and care-worn at thirty, and who still managed to live to an old age. He was indefinably glad that Easter had escaped such a fate. When he left the cabin, the old man called after him from the door:

"Thar's goin' to be a shootin'-match among the boys to-morrer, 'n' I jedge that Easter 'll be on hand. She al'ays is."

"Is that so?" said Clayton. "Well, I'll look out for it."

The old mountaineer lowered his voice.

"Ye hain't thinkin' about takin' a wife, air ye?"

"No, no!"

"Well, ef ye air," said the old man, slowly, "I'm a-thinkin' yu'll have to buck up ag'in Sherd Raines, fer ef I hain't like a goose a-pickin' o' grass by moonshine, Sherd air atter the gal fer hisself, not fer the Lord. Yes," he continued, after a short, dry laugh; "'n' mebbe ye'll hav to keep an eye open fer old Bill. They say that he air mighty low down, 'n' kind o' sorry 'n' skeery, for I reckon Sherd Raines hev told him he hav got to pay the penalty fer takin' a human life; but I wouldn't sot much on his bein' sorry ef he was mad at me and had licker in him. He hates furriners, and he has a crazy idee that they is all raiders 'n' lookin' fer him."

"I don't think I'll bother him," said Clayton, turning away with a laugh. "Good-night!" With a little cackle of incredulity, the old man closed the door. The camp had sunk now to perfect quiet; but for the faint notes of a banjo far up the glen, not a sound trembled on the night air.

The rim of the moon was just visible above the mountain on which Easter—what a pretty name that was!—had flashed upon his vision with such theatric effect. As its brilliant light came slowly down the dark mountain-side, the mists seemed to loosen their white arms, and to creep away like ghosts mistaking the light for dawn. With the base of the mountain in dense shadow, its crest, uplifted through the vapors, seemed poised in the air at a startling height. Yet it was near the crest that he had met her. Clayton paused a moment, when he reached his door, to look again. Where in that cloud-land could she live?

III

WHEN the great bell struck the hour of the next noon, mountaineers with long rifles across their shoulders were moving through the camp. The glen opened into a valley, which, blocked on the east by Pine Mountain, was thus shut in on every side by wooded heights. Here the marksmen gathered. All were mountaineers, lank, bearded men, coatless for the most part, and dressed in brown home-made jeans, slouched, formless hats, and high, coarse boots. Sun and wind had tanned their faces to sympathy, in color, with their clothes, which had the dun look of the soil. They seemed peculiarly a race of the soil, to have sprung as they were from the earth, which had left indelible stains upon them. All carried long rifles, old-fashioned and home-made, some even with flint-locks. It was Saturday, and many of their wives had come with them to the camp. These stood near, huddled into a listless group, with their faces half hidden in check bonnets of various colors. A barbaric love of color was apparent in bonnet, shawl, and gown, and surprisingly in contrast with such crudeness of taste was a face when fully seen, so modest was it. The features were always delicately wrought, and softened sometimes by a look of patient suffering almost into refinement.

On the other side of the contestants were the people of the camp, a few miners with pipes lounging on the ground, and women and girls, who returned the furtive glances of the mountain women with stares of curiosity and low laughter.

Clayton had been delayed by his work, and the match was already going on when he reached the grounds.

"You've missed mighty fine shootin'," said Uncle Tommy Brooks, who was squatted on the ground near the group of marksmen. "Sherd's been a-beatin' ever'body. I'm afeard Easter hain't a-comin'. The match is 'most over now. Ef she'd been here, I don't think Sherd would 'a' got the ch'ice parts o' that beef so easy."

"Which is he?" asked Clayton.

"That tall feller thar loadin' his gun."

"What did you say his name was?"

"Sherd Raines, the feller that's goin' to be our circuit-rider."

He remembered the peculiar name. So this

24

was Easter's lover. Clayton looked at the young mountaineer, curiously at first, and then with growing interest. His quiet air of authority among his fellows was like a birthright; it seemed assumed and accepted unconsciously. His face was smooth, and he was fuller in figure than the rest, but still sinewy and lank, though not awkward; his movements were too quick and decisive for that. With a casual glance Clayton had wondered what secret influence could have turned to spiritual things a man so merely animal-like in face and physique; but when the mountaineer thrust back his hat, elemental strength and seriousness were apparent in the square brow, the steady eye, the poise of the head, and in lines around the strong mouth and chin in which the struggle for self-mastery had been traced.

As the mountaineer thrust his ramrod back into its casing, he glanced at the woods behind Clayton, and said something to his companions. They, too, raised their eyes, and at the same moment the old mountaineer plucked Clayton by the sleeve.

" Thar comes Easter now."

The girl had just emerged from the edge of the forest, and with a rifle on one shoulder and a bullet-pouch and powder-horn swung from the other, was slowly coming down the path.

"Why, how air ye, Easter?" cried the old man, heartily. "Goin' to shoot, air ye? I 'lowed ye wouldn't miss this. Ye air mighty late, though."

"Oh, I only wanted a turkey," said the girl.

"Well, I'm a-comin' up to eat dinner with ye to-morrer," he answered, with a laugh, "fer I know ye'll git one. Y'u're on hand fer most o' the matches now. *Wild* turkeys must be a-gittin' skeerce."

The girl smiled, showing a row of brilliant teeth between her thin, red lips, and, without answering, moved toward the group of mountain women. Clayton had raised his hand to his hat when the old man addressed her, but he dropped it quickly to his side in no little embarrassment when the girl carelessly glanced over him with no sign of recognition. Her rifle was an old flint-lock of light build, but nearly six feet in length, with a shade of rusty tin two feet long fastened to the barrel to prevent the sunlight from affecting the marksman's aim. She wore a man's hat, which, with unintentional coquetry, was perched on one side of her head. Her hair was short, and fell as it pleased about her neck. She was bare-footed, and apparently clad in a single garment, a blue homespun gown, gathered loosely at her uncorseted waist, and showing the outline of the bust and every movement of the tall, supple form beneath. Her appearance had quickened the interest of the spectators, and apparently was a disturbing influence among the contestants, who were gathered together, evidently in dispute. From their glances Clayton saw that Easter was the subject of it.

" I guess they don't want her to shoot—them that hain't won nothin'," said Uncle Tommy.

" She hev come in late," Clayton heard one say, " 'n' she oughtn' to shoot. Thar hain't no chance shootin' ag'in her noways, 'n' I'm in favor o' barrin' her out."

" Oh no; let her shoot "—the voice was Raines's. " Thar hain't nothin' but a few turkeys left, 'n' ye'd better bar out the gun 'stid o' the gal, anyway, fer that gun kin outshoot anything in the mountains."

The girl had been silently watching the group as if puzzled; and when Raines spoke her face tightened with sudden decision, and she strode swiftly toward them in time to overhear the young mountaineer's last words.

" So hit's the gun, is hit, Sherd Raines? " The crowd turned, and Raines shrank a little as the girl faced him with flashing eyes. " So hit's the gun, is hit? Hit *is* a good gun, but y ought to be ashamed to take all the credit 'w y from me. But ef you air so *sartain* hit's the

27

gun," she continued, " I'll shoot yourn, 'n' y'u kin hev mine ef I don't beat ye with yer own gun."

" Good fer you, Easter!" shouted the old mountaineer.

Raines had recovered himself, and was looking at the girl seriously. Several of his companions urged him aloud to accept the challenge, but he paid no heed to them. He seemed to be debating the question with himself, and a moment later he said, quietly:

" 'N' you kin hev mine ef I don't beat you."

This was all he said, but he kept his eyes fixed on the girl's face; and when, with a defiant glance, she turned toward the mountain women, he followed and stopped her.

" Easter," Clayton heard him say, in a low, slow voice, " I was tryin' to git ye a chance to shoot, fer ye hev been winnin' so much that it's hard to git up a match when ye air in it." The hard look on the girl's face remained unchanged, and the mountaineer continued, firmly:

" 'N' I told the truth; fer ef ye pin me down, I do think hit *is* the gun."

" Jes you wait 'n' see," answered the girl, shortly, and Raines, after a questioning look, rejoined the group.

" I won't take the gun ef I win it," he said

28

to them; "but she air gittin' too set up an' proud, 'n' I'm goin' to do my best to take her down a bit."

There was nothing boastful or malicious in his manner or speech, and nobody doubted that he would win, for there were few marksmen in the mountains his equals, and he would have the advantage of using his own gun.

"Look hyeh," said a long, thin mountaineer, coming up to the group, "thar ain't but one turkey left, 'n' I'd like to know what we air goin' to shoot at ef Sherd 'n' Easter gits a crack at him."

In the interest of the match no one had thought of that, and a moment of debate followed, which Clayton ended by stepping forward.

"I'll furnish a turkey for the rest of you," he said.

The girl turned when he spoke and gave him a quick glance, but averted her eyes instantly.

Clayton's offer was accepted, and the preliminary trial to decide who should shoot first at the turkey was begun. Every detail was watched with increasing interest. A piece of white paper marked with two concentric circles was placed sixty yards away, and Raines won with a bullet in the inner circle. The girl had missed both, and the mountaineer offered her two more shots to accustom herself to the gun. She accepted, and smiled a little triumphantly as she touched the outer circle with one bullet and placed the other almost in the centre. It was plain that the two were evenly matched, and several shouts of approval came from the crowd. The turkey was hobbled to a stake at the same distance, and both were to fire at its head, with the privilege of shooting at fifty yards if no rest were taken.

Raines shot first without rest, and, as he missed, the girl followed his example. The turkey dozed on in the sunlight, undisturbed by either. The mountaineer was vexed. With his powerful face set determinedly, he lay down flat on the ground, and, resting his rifle over a small log, took an inordinately long and careful aim. The rifle cracked, the turkey bobbed its head unhurt, and the marksman sprang to his feet with an exclamation of surprise and chagrin. As he loaded the gun and gravely handed it to the girl, the excitement grew intense. The crowd pressed close. The stolid faces of the mountaineer women, thrust from their bonnets, became almost eager with interest. Raines, quiet and composed as he was, looked anxious. All eyes followed every movement of the girl as she coolly stretched her long, active figure on the ground, drew her dress close about it, and, throwing her yellow hair over her face to shade her eyes from the slanting sunlight, placed her cheek against the stock of the gun. A long suspense followed. A hush almost of solemnity fell upon the crowd.

"Why don't the gal shoot?" asked a voice, impatiently.

Clayton saw what the matter was, and, stepping toward her, said quietly, "You forgot to set the trigger."

The girl's face colored. Again her eye glanced along the barrel, a puff of smoke flew from the gun, and a shout came from every pair of lips as the turkey leaped into the air and fell, beating the ground with its wings. In an instant a young mountaineer had rushed forward and seized it, and, after a glance, dropped it with a yell of triumph.

"Shot plum' through the eyes!" he shouted. "Shot plum' through the eyes!"

The girl arose, and handed the gun back to Raines.

"Keep hit," he said, steadily. "Hit's yourn."

"I don't want the gun," she said, "but I did want that turkey—'n' "—a little tauntingly —"I did want to beat you, Sherd Raines."

The mountaineer's face flushed and darkened, but he said nothing. He took no part in the shooting that followed, and when, after the match was over, the girl, with her rifle on one shoulder and the turkey over the other, turned up the mountain path, Clayton saw him follow her.

IV

A FORTNIGHT later Clayton, rifle in hand, took the same path. It was late in May. The leafage was luxuriant, and the mountains, wooded to the tops, seemed overspread with great, shaggy rugs of green. The woods were resonant with song-birds, and the dew dripped and sparkled wherever a shaft of sunlight pierced the thick leaves. Late violets hid shyly under canopies of May-apple; bunches of blue and of white anemone nodded from under fallen trees, and water ran like hidden music everywhere. Slowly the valley and the sound of its life—the lowing of cattle, the clatter at the mines, the songs of the negroes at work—sank beneath him. The chorus of birds dwindled until only the cool, flute-like notes of a wood-thrush rose faintly from below. Up he went, winding around great oaks, fallen trunks, loose bowlders, and threatening cliffs until light glimmered whitely between the boles of the trees. From a gap where he paused to rest, a " fire-scald " was visible close to the crest of the adjoining mountain. It was filled with the

33

charred, ghost-like trunks of trees that had been burned standing. Easter's home must be near that, Clayton thought, and he turned toward it by a path that ran along the top of the mountain. After a few hundred yards the path swerved sharply through a dense thicket, and Clayton stopped in wonder.

Some natural agent had hollowed the mountain, leaving a level plateau of several acres. The earth had fallen away from a great sombre cliff of solid rock, and clinging like a swallow's nest in a cleft of this was the usual rude cabin of a mountaineer. The face of the rock was dark with vines, and the cabin was protected as by a fortress. But one way of approach was possible, and that straight to the porch. From the cliff the vines had crept to roof and chimney, and were waving their tendrils about a thin blue spiral of smoke. The cabin was gray and tottering with age. Above the porch on the branches of an apple-tree hung leaves that matched in richness of tint the thick moss on the rough shingles. Under it an old woman sat spinning, and a hound lay asleep at her feet. Easter was nowhere to be seen, but her voice came from below him in a loud tone of command; and presently she appeared from behind a knoll, above which the thatched roof of a stable was visible, and slowly ascended the path to the house. She had evidently just finished work, for a plough stood in the last furrow of the field, and the fragrance of freshly turned earth was in the air. On the porch she sank wearily into a low chair, and, folding her hands, looked away to the mountains.

Clayton climbed the crumbling fence. A dead twig snapped, and, startled by the sound, the girl began to rise; but, giving him one quick, sharp look, dropped her eyes to her hands, and remained motionless.

" Good morning," said Clayton, lifting his hat. The girl did not raise her face. The wheel stopped, and the spinner turned her head.

" How air ye? " she said, with ready hospitality. " Come in an' hev a cheer."

" No, thank you," he answered, a little embarrassed by Easter's odd behavior. " May I get some water? "

" Sartinly," said the old woman, looking him over curiously. " Easter, go git some fresh."

The girl started to rise, but Clayton, picking up the bucket, said, quickly:

" Oh no; I won't trouble you. I see the spring," he added, noticing a tiny stream that trickled from a fissure at the base of the cliff.

" Who air that feller, Easter? " the mother asked, in a low voice, when Clayton was out of hearing.

35

"One o' them furriners who hev come into Injun Creek," was the indifferent reply.

"That's splendid water," said Clayton, returning. "May I give you some?" The old woman shook her head. Easter's eyes were still on the mountains, and apparently she had not heard him.

"Hit air good water," said the mother. "That spring never does go dry. You better come in and rest a spell. I suppose ye air from the mines?" she added, as she turned to resume spinning.

"Yes," answered Clayton. "There is good hunting around here, isn't there?" he went on, feeling that some explanation was due for his sudden arrival away up in that lone spot.

There was no answer. Easter did not look toward him, and the spinning stopped.

"Whut d'you say?" asked the old woman. Clayton repeated his question.

"Thar used to be prime huntin' in these parts when my dad cleared off this spot more'n fifty year ago, but the varmints hev mostly been killed out. But Easter kin tell you better'n I kin, for she does all our huntin', 'n' she kin outshoot 'mos' any man in the mountains."

"Yes; I saw her shoot at the match the other day down at the mines."

"Did ye?"—a smile of pleasure broke over

36

the old woman's face—"whar she beat Sherd Raines? Sherd wanted to mortify *her*, but she mortified *him*, I reckon."

The girl did not join in her mother's laugh, though the corners of her mouth twitched faintly.

" I like shooting, myself," said Clayton. " I would go into a match, but I'm afraid I wouldn't have much chance."

" I reckon not, with that short thing? " said the old woman, pointing at his repeating-rifle. " Would ye shoot with that? "

" Oh, yes," answered Clayton, smiling; " it shoots very well."

" How fer? "

" Oh, a long way."

A huge shadow swept over the house, thrown by a buzzard sailing with magnificent ease high above them. Thinking that he might disturb its flight, Clayton rose and cocked his rifle.

" Ye're not going to shoot at that? " said the old woman, grinning. The girl had looked toward him at last, with a smile of faint derision.

Clayton took aim quickly and fired. The huge bird sank as though hit, curved downward, and with one flap of his great wings sailed on.

" Well, ef I didn't think ye had hit him! "

said the old woman, in amazement. " You kin shoot, fer a fac'."

Easter's attention was gained at last. For the first time she looked straight at him, and her little smile of derision had given way to a look of mingled curiosity and respect.

" I expected only to scare him," said Clayton. " The gun will carry twice that far."

" Hit's jest as well ye didn't hit him," said the old woman. " Hit air five dollars fine to kill a buzzard around hyeh. I'd never thought that little thing could shoot."

" It shoots several times," said Clayton.

" Hit does *whut?*"

" Like a pistol," he explained, and, rising, he directed several shots in quick succession at a dead tree in the ploughed field. At each shot a puff of dust came almost from the same spot.

When he turned, Easter had risen to her feet in astonishment, and the mother was laughing long and loudly.

" Don't ye wish ye had a gun like that, Easter? " she cried.

Clayton turned quickly to the girl, and began explaining the mechanism of the gun to her, without appearing to notice her embarrassment, for she shrank perceptibly when he spoke to her.

" Won't you let me see your gun? " he asked.

She brought out the old flint-lock, and handed it to him almost timidly.

"This is very interesting," he said. " I never saw one like it before."

"Thar hain't but one more jest like that in the mountains," said the old woman, " 'n' Easter's got that. My dad made 'em both."

"How would you like to trade one for mine, if you have two?" said Clayton to the girl. "I'll give you all my cartridges to boot."

The girl looked at her mother with hesitation. Clayton saw that both wondered what he could want with the gun, and he added:

"I'd like to have it to take home with me. It would be a great curiosity."

"Well," said the mother, "you kin hev one ef ye want hit, and think the trade's fa'r."

Clayton insisted, and the trade was made. The old woman resumed spinning. The girl took her seat in the low chair, holding her new treasure in her lap, with her eyes fixed on it, and occasionally running one brown hand down its shining barrel. Clayton watched her. She had given no sign whatever that she had ever seen him before, and yet a curious change had come over her. Her imperious manner had yielded to a singular reserve and timidity. The peculiar beauty of the girl struck him now with unusual force. Her profile was remarkably regular and

39

delicate; her mouth small, resolute, and sensitive; heavy, dark lashes shaded her downcast eyes; and her brow suggested a mentality that he felt a strong desire to test. Her feet were small, and so were her quick, nervous hands, which were still finely shaped, in spite of the hard usage that had left them brown and callous. He wondered if she was really as lovely as she seemed; if his standard might not have been affected by his long stay in the mountains; if her picturesque environment might not have influenced his judgment. He tried to imagine her daintily slippered, clad in white, with her loose hair gathered in a Psyche knot; or in evening dress, with arms and throat bare; but the pictures were difficult to make. He liked her best as she was, in perfect physical sympathy with the natural phases about her; as much a part of them as tree, plant, or flower, embodying the freedom, grace, and beauty of nature as well and as unconsciously as they. He questioned whether she hardly felt herself to be apart from them; and, of course, she as little knew her kinship to them.

She had lifted her eyes now, and had fixed them with tender thoughtfulness on the mountains. What did she see in the scene before her, he wondered: the deep valley, brilliant with early sunshine; the magnificent sweep of wooded slopes; Pine Mountain and the peak-like Narrows, where through it the river had worn its patient way; and the Cumberland Range, lying like a cloud against the horizon, and bluer and softer than the sky above it. He longed to know what her thoughts were; if in them there might be a hint of what he hoped to find. Probably she could not tell them, should he ask her, so unconscious was she of her mental life, whatever that might be. Indeed, she seemed scarcely to know of her own existence; there was about her a simplicity to which he had felt himself rise only in the presence of the spirit about some lonely mountain-top or in the heart of deep woods. Her gaze was not vacant, not listless, but the pensive look of a sensitive child, and Clayton let himself fancy that there was in it an unconscious love of the beauty before her, and of its spiritual suggestiveness a slumbering sense, perhaps easily awakened. Perhaps he might awaken it.

The drowsy hum of the spinning-wheel ceased suddenly, and his dream was shattered. He wondered how long they had sat there saying nothing, and how long the silence might continue. Easter, he believed, would never address him. Even the temporary intimacy that the barter of the gun had brought about was gone. The girl seemed lost in unconsciousness. The

mother had gone to her loom, and was humming
softly to herself as she passed the shuttle to and
fro. Clayton turned for an instant to watch her,
and the rude background, which he had forgotten, thrust every unwelcome detail upon his attention: the old cabin, built of hewn logs, held
together by wooden pin and augur-hole, and
shingled with rough boards; the dark, window-
less room; the unplastered walls; the beds with
old-fashioned high posts, mattresses of straw,
and cords instead of slats; the home-made chairs
with straight backs, tipped with carved knobs;
the mantel filled with utensils and overhung with
bunches of drying herbs; a ladder with half a
dozen smooth-worn steps leading to the loft;
and a wide, deep fireplace—the only suggestion
of cheer and comfort in the gloomy interior.
An open porch connected the single room with
the kitchen. Here, too, were suggestions of
daily duties. The mother's face told a tale of
hardship and toil, and there was the plough in
the furrow, and the girl's calloused hands folded
in her lap. With a thrill of compassion Clayton
turned to her. What a pity! what a pity! Just
now her face had the peace of a child's; but
when aroused, an electric fire burned from her
calm eyes and showed the ardent temperament
that really lay beneath. If she were quick and
sympathetic—and she must be, he thought—

who could tell how rich the development possible for her?

"You hain't seen much of this country, I reckon. You hain't been here afore?"

The mother had broken the silence at last.

"No," said Clayton; "but I like it very much."

"Do ye?" she asked, in surprise. "Why, I 'lowed you folks from the settlemints thought hit was mighty scraggy down hyeh."

"Oh no. These mountains and woods are beautiful, and I never saw lovelier beech-trees. The coloring of their trunks is so exquisite, and the shade is so fine," he concluded, lamely, noticing a blank look on the old woman's face. To his delight the girl, half turned toward him, was listening with puzzled interest.

"Well," said the old woman, "beeches is beautiful to me when they has mast enough to feed the hogs."

Carried back to his train of speculations, Clayton started at this abrupt deliverance. There was a suspicion of humor in the old woman's tone that showed an appreciation of their different standpoints. It was lost on Clayton, however, for his attention had been caught by the word "mast," which, by some accident, he had never heard before.

"Mast," he asked, "what is that?"

43

The girl looked toward him in amazement, and burst into a low, suppressed laugh. Her mother explained the word, and all laughed heartily.

Clayton soon saw that his confession of ignorance was a lucky accident. It brought Easter and himself nearer common ground. She felt that there was something, after all, that she could teach him. She had been overpowered by his politeness and deference and his unusual language, and, not knowing what they meant, was overcome by a sense of her inferiority. The incident gave him the key to his future conduct. A moment later she looked up covertly, and, meeting his eyes, laughed again. The ice was broken. He began to wonder if she really had noticed him so little at their first meeting as not to recognize him, or if her indifference or reserve had prevented her from showing the recognition. He pulled out his note-book and began sketching rapidly, conscious that the girl was watching him. When he finished, he rose, picking up the old flint-lock.

" Won't ye stay and hev some dinner? " asked the old woman.

" No, thank you."

" Come ag'in," she said, cordially, adding the mountaineer's farewell, " I wish ye well."

" Thank you, I will. Good-day."

44

As he passed the girl he paused a moment and dropped the paper into her lap. It was a rude sketch of their first meeting, the bull coming at him like a tornado. The color came to her face, and when Clayton turned the corner of the house he heard her laughing.

"What you laughin' at, Easter?" asked the mother, stopping her work and looking around.

For answer the girl rose and walked into the house, hiding the paper in her bosom. The old woman watched her narrowly.

"I never seed ye afeard of a man afore," she said to herself. "No, nur so tickled 'bout one, nother. Well, he air as accommodatin' a feller as I ever see, ef he air a furriner. But he was a fool to swop his gun fer hern."

V

THEREAFTER Clayton saw the girl
whenever possible. If she came to the
camp, he walked up the mountain with her. No
idle day passed that he did not visit the cabin,
and it was not long before he found himself
strangely interested. Her beauty and fearless-
ness had drawn him at first; her indifference and
stolidity had piqued him; and now the shyness
that displaced these was inconsistent and puz-
zling. This he set himself deliberately at work
to remove, and the conscious effort gave a peculiar piquancy to their intercourse. He had
learned the secret of association with the mountaineers—to be as little unlike them as possible
—and he put the knowledge into practice. He
discarded coat and waistcoat, wore a slouched
hat, and went unshaven for weeks. He avoided
all conventionalities, and was as simple in manner and speech as possible. Often when talking
with Easter, her face was blankly unresponsive,
and a question would sometimes leave her in
confused silence. He found it necessary to use
the simplest Anglo-Saxon words, and he soon

46

fell into many of the quaint expressions of the
mountaineers and their odd, slow way of speech.
This course was effective, and in time the shyness wore away and left between them a com-
radeship as pleasant as unique. Sometimes they
took long walks together on the mountains.
This was contrary to mountain etiquette, but they
were remote even from the rude conventionalities of the life below them. They even went
hunting together, and Easter had the joy of a
child when she discovered her superiority to
Clayton in woodcraft and in the use of a rifle.
If he could tell her the names of plants and
flowers they found, and how they were akin, she
could show him where they grew. If he could
teach her a little more about animals and their
habits than she already knew, he had always to
follow her in the search for game. Their fel-
lowship was, in consequence, never more complete than when they were roaming the woods.
In them Easter was at home, and her ardent
nature came to the surface like a poetic glow
from her buoyant health and beauty. Then appeared all that was wayward and elfin-like in her
character, and she would be as playful, wilful,
evanescent as a wood-spirit. Sometimes, when
they were separated, she would lead him into a
ravine by imitating a squirrel or a wild-turkey,
and, as he crept noiselessly along with bated

breath and eyes peering eagerly through the tree-tops or the underbrush, she would step like a dryad from behind some tree at his side, with a ringing laugh at his discomfiture. Again, she might startle him by running lightly along the fallen trunk of a tree that lay across a torrent, or, in a freak of wilfulness, would let herself down the bare face of some steep cliff. If he scolded her, she laughed. If he grew angry, she was serious instantly, and once she fell to weeping and fled home. He followed her, but she barricaded herself in her room in the loft, and would not be coaxed down. The next day she had forgotten that she was angry.

Her mother showed no surprise at any of her moods. Easter was not like other " gals," she said; she had always been " quar," and she reckoned would " al'ays be that way." She objected in no wise to Clayton's intimacy with her. The " furriner," she told Raines, was the only man who had ever been able to manage her, and if she wanted Easter to do anything " ag'in her will, she went to him fust "—a simple remark that threw the mountaineer into deep thoughtfulness.

Indeed, this sense of power that Clayton felt over the wilful, passionate creature thrilled him with more pleasure than he would have been willing to admit; at the same time it suggested to him a certain responsibility. Why not make use of it, and a good use? The girl was perhaps deplorably ignorant, could do but little more than read and write; but she was susceptible of development, and at times apparently conscious of the need of it and desirous for it. Once he had carried her a handful of violets, and thereafter an old pitcher that stood on a shelf blossomed every day with wild-flowers. He had transplanted a vine from the woods and taught her to train it over the porch, and the first hint of tenderness he found in her nature was in the care of that plant. He had taken her a book full of pictures and fashion-plates, and he had noticed a quick and ingenious adoption of some of its hints in her dress.

One afternoon, as he lay on his bed in a darkened corner of his room, a woman's shadow passed across the wall, returned, and a moment later he saw Easter's face at the window. He had lain quiet, and watched her while her wondering eyes roved from one object to another, until they were fastened with a long, intent look on a picture that stood upon a table near the window. He stirred, and her face melted away instantly. A few days later he was sitting with Easter and Raines at the cabin. The mother was at the other end of the porch, talking to a neigh-

bor who had stopped to rest on his way across
the mountains.

"Easter air a-gettin' high notions," she was
saying, "'n' she air a-spendin' her savin's, 'n'
all mine she kin git hold of, to buy fixin's
at the commissary. She must hev white crock-
ery, 'n' towels, 'n' newfangled forks, 'n' sich-
like." A conscious flush came into the girl's
face, and she rose hastily and went into the
house.

"I was afeard," continued the mother, "that
she would hev her hair cut short, 'n' be a-flyin'
with ribbons, 'n' spangled out like a rainbow,
like old 'Lige Hicks's gal, ef I hadn't heerd the
furriner tell her it was 'beastly.' Thar ain't no
fear now, fer what that furriner don't like,
Easter don't nother."

For an instant the mountaineer's eyes had
flashed on Clayton, but when the latter, a trifle
embarrassed, looked up, Raines apparently had
heard nothing. Easter did not reappear until
the mountaineer was gone.

There were other hopeful signs. Whenever
Clayton spoke of his friends, she always listened
eagerly, and asked innumerable questions about
them. If his attention was caught by any queer
custom or phrase of the mountain dialect, she
was quick to ask in return how he would say
the same thing, and what the custom was in the

" settlemints." She even made feeble attempts
to model her own speech after his.

In a conscious glow that he imagined was
philanthropy, Clayton began his task of elevation. She was not so ignorant as he had supposed. Apparently she had been taught by
somebody, but when asked by whom, she hesitated answering, and he had taken it for granted
that what she knew she had puzzled out alone.
He was astonished by her quickness, her docil-
ity, and the passionate energy with which she
worked. Her instant obedience to every suggestion, her trust in every word he uttered, made
him acutely and at times uncomfortably conscious of his responsibility. At the same time
there was in the task something of the pleasure
that a young sculptor feels when, for the first
time, the clay begins to yield obedience to his
fingers, and something of the delight that must
have thrilled Pygmalion when he saw his statue
tremulous with conscious life.

VI

THE possibility of lifting the girl above her own people, and of creating a spirit of discontent that might embitter her whole life, had occurred to Clayton; but at such moments the figure of Raines came into the philanthropic picture forming slowly in his mind, and his conscience was quieted. He could see them together; the gradual change that Easter would bring about in him, the influence of the two on their fellows. The mining-camp grew into a town with a modest church on the outskirts, and a cottage where Raines and Easter were installed. They stood between the old civilization and the new, understanding both, and protecting the native strength of the one from the vices of the other, and training it after more breadth and refinement. But Raines and Easter did not lend themselves to the picture so readily, and gradually it grew vague and shadowy, and the figure of the mountaineer was blurred.

Clayton did not bring harmony to the two. At first he saw nothing of the mountaineer, and when they met at the cabin Raines remained only a short time. If Easter cared for him at all, she did not show it. How he was regarded by the mother, Clayton had learned long ago, when, in answer to one of his questions, she had said, with a look at Easter, that " Raines was the likeliest young feller in them mountains "; that " he knew morn'n anybody round thar "; that " he had spent a year in the settlemints, was mighty religious, and would one day be a circuit-rider. Anyhow," she concluded, " he was a mighty good friend o' theirn."

But as for Easter, she treated him with unvarying indifference, though Clayton noticed she was more quiet and reserved in the mountaineer's presence; and, what was unintelligible to him, she refused to speak of her studies when Raines was at the cabin, and warned her mother with an angry frown when the latter began telling the mountaineer of "whut a change had come over Easter, and how she reckoned the gal was a-gittin' eddicated enough fer to teach anybody in the mountains, she was a-larnin' so much."

After that little incident, he met Raines at the cabin oftener. The mountaineer was always taciturn, though he listened closely when anything was said, and even when addressed by Easter's mother his attention, Clayton noticed, was fixed on Easter and himself. He felt that

53

he was being watched, and it irritated him. He had tried to be friendly with the mountaineer, but his advances were received with a reserve that was almost suspicion. As time went on, the mountaineer's visits increased in frequency and in length, and at last one night he stayed so long that, for the first time, Clayton left him there.

Neither spoke after the young engineer was gone. The mountaineer sat looking closely at Easter, who was listlessly watching the moon as it rose above the Cumberland Range and brought into view the wavering outline of Pine Mountain and the shadowed valley below. It was evident from his face and his eyes, which glowed with the suppressed fire of some powerful emotion within, that he had remained for a purpose; and when he rose and said, " I reckon I better be a-goin', Easter," his voice was so unnatural that the girl looked up quickly.

" Hit air late," she said, after a slight pause.

His face flushed, but he set his lips and caught the back of his chair, as though to steady himself.

" I reckon," he said, with slow bitterness, " that hit would 'a' been early long as the furriner was hyeh."

The girl was roused instantly, but she said nothing, and he continued, in a determined tone:

54

"Easter, thar's a good deal I've wanted to say to ye fer a long time, but I hev kept a-puttin' hit off until I'm afeard maybe hit air too late. But I'm a-goin' to say hit now, and I want ye to listen." He cleared his throat huskily. "Do ye know, Easter, what folks in the mountains is a-sayin'?"

The girl's quick insight told her what was coming, and her face hardened.

"Have ye ever knowed me, Sherd Raines, to keer what folks in the mountains say? I reckon ye mean as how they air a-talkin' about me?"

"That's what I mean," said the mountaineer—"you 'n' *him.*"

"Whut air they a-sayin'?" she asked, defiantly. Raines watched her narrowly.

"They air a-sayin' as how he air a-comin' up here mighty often; as how Easter Hicks, who hev never keered fer no man, air in love with this furriner from the settlemints."

The girl reddened, in spite of her assumed indifference.

"They say, too, as how he air not in love with her, 'n' that somebody oughter warn Easter that he air not a-meanin' good to her. You hev been seed a-walkin' in the mountains together."

"Who seed me?" she asked, with quick suspicion. The mountaineer hesitated.

"I hev," he said, doggedly.

The girl's anger, which had been kindling against her gossiping fellows, blazed out against Raines.

"You've been watchin' me," she said, angrily. "Who give ye the right to do it? What call hev ye to come hyar and tell me whut folks is a-sayin'? Is it any o' *yo'* business? I want to tell ye, Sherd Raines"—her utterance grew thick—"that I kin take keer o' myself; that I don't keer what folks say; 'n' I want ye to keep away from me. 'N' ef I sees ye a-hangin' round 'n' a-spyin', ye'll be sorry fer it." Her eyes blazed, she had risen and drawn herself straight, and her hands were clinched.

The mountaineer stood motionless. "Thar's another who's seed ye," he said, quietly—"up thar," pointing to a wooded mountain, the top of which was lost in mist. The girl's attitude changed instantly into vague alarm, and her eyes flashed upon Raines as though they would sear their way into the meaning hidden in his quiet face. Gradually his motive seemed to become clear, and she advanced a step toward him.

"So you've found out whar dad is a-hidin'?" she said, her voice tremulous with rage and scorn. "'N' ye air mean and sorry enough to some hyeh 'n' tell me ye'll give him up to the law ef I don't knuckle down 'n' do what ye wants me?"

She paused a moment. Was her suspicion correct? Why did he not speak? She did not really believe what she said. Could it be true? Her nostrils quivered; she tried to speak again, but her voice was choked with passion. With a sudden movement she snatched her rifle from its place, and the steel flashed in the moonlight and ceased in a shining line straight at the mountaineer's breast.

"Look hyeh, Sherd Raines," she said, in low, unsteady tones, "I know you air religious, 'n' I know as how, when y'u give yer word, you'll do what you say. Now, I want ye to hold up yer right hand and sw'ar that you'll never tell a livin' soul that you know whar dad is a-hidin'."

Raines did not turn his face, which was as emotionless as stone.

"Air ye goin' to sw'ar?" she asked, with fierce impatience. Without looking at her, he began to speak—very slowly:

"Do ye think I'm fool enough to try to gain yer good-will by a-tellin' on yer dad? We were on the mountains, him 'n' me, we seed you 'n' the furriner. Yer dad thought hit was a spy, 'n' he whipped up his gun 'n' would 'a' shot him dead in his tracks ef I hadn't hindered him.

57

Does that look like I wanted to hurt the fur-riner? I hev knowed yer dad was up in the mountains all the time, 'n' I hev been a-totin' things fer him to eat. Does that look like I wanted to hand him over to the law?"

The girl had let the rifle fall. Moving away, she stood leaning on it in the shadow, looking down.

"You want to know what call I hev to watch ye, 'n' see that no harm comes to ye. Yer dad give me the right. You know how he hates fur-riners, 'n' whut he would do ef he happened to run across this furriner atter he has been drinkin'. I'm a-meddlin' because I hev told him that I am goin' to take keer o' ye, 'n' I mean to do it—ef ye hates me fer it. I'm a-watchin' ye, Easter," he continued, "'n' I want ye to know it. I knowed the furriner begun comin' here 'cause ye air not like gals in the settlemints. Y'u air as cur'us to him as one o' them bugs an' sich-like that he's always a-pickin' up in the woods. I hevn't said nuthin' to yer dad, fer fear o' his harmin' the furriner; but I hev seed that ye like him, an' hit's time now fer me to meddle. Ef he was in love with ye, do ye think he would marry ye? I hev been in the settle-mints. Folks thar air not as we citizens air. They air bigoted 'n' high-heeled, 'n' they look down on us. I tell ye, too—'n' hit air fer yer

58

own good—he air in love with somebody in the
settlemints. I hev heerd it, 'n' I hev seed him
a-lookin' at a picter in his room ez a man don't
look at his sister. They say hit's her.

"Thar's one thing more, Easter," he concluded, as he stepped from the porch. "He is
a-goin' away. I heard him say it yestiddy.
What will ye do when he's gone ef ye lets yerself git to thinkin' so much of him now? I've
warned ye now, Easter, fer yer own good,
though ye mought think I'm a-workin' fer myself. But I know I hev done whut I ought.
I've warned ye, 'n' ye kin do whut ye please, but
I'm a-watchin' ye."

The girl said nothing, but stood rigid, with
eyes wide open and face tense, as the mountaineer's steps died away. She was bewildered by
the confused emotions that swayed her. Why
had she not indignantly denied that she was in
love with the "furriner"? Raines had not
hinted it as a suspicion. He had spoken it outright as a fact, and he must have thought that
her silence confirmed it. He had said that the
"furriner" cared nothing for her, and had
dared to tell her that she was in love with him.
Her cheeks began to burn. She would call him
back and tell him that she cared no more for the
"furriner" than she did for him. She started
from the steps, but paused, straining her eyes

through the darkness. It was too late, and, with a helpless little cry, she began pacing the porch. She had scarcely heard what was said after the mountaineer's first accusation, so completely had that enthralled her mind; now fragments came back to her. There was something about a picture—ah! she remembered that picture. Passing through the camp one afternoon, she had glanced in at a window and had seen a rifle once her own. Turning in rapid wonder about the room, her eye lighted upon a picture on a table near the window. She had felt the refined beauty of the girl, and it had impressed her with the same timidity that Clayton had when she first knew him. Fascinated, she had looked till a movement in the room made her shrink away. But the face had clung in her memory ever since, and now it came before her vividly. Clayton was in love with her. Well, what did that matter to *her?*

There was more that Raines said. " Goin' away." Raines meant the " furriner," of course. How did he know? Why had Clayton not told her? She did not believe it. But why not? He had once told her that he would go away some time; why not now? But why—why did not Clayton tell her? Perhaps he was going to *her.* She almost stretched out her hands in a sudden, fierce desire to clutch the round throat and sink her nails into the soft flesh that rose before her mind. She had forgotten that he had ever told her that he must go away, so little had it impressed her at the time. She had never thought of a possible change in their relations or in their lives. She tried to think what her life would be after he was gone, and she was frightened; she could not imagine her old life resumed. When Clayton came, it was as though she had risen from sleep in a dream, and had lived in it thereafter without questioning its reality. Into his hands she had delivered her life and herself with the undoubting faith of a child. She had never thought of their relations at all. Now the awakening had come. The dream was shattered. For the first time her eye was turned inward, where a flood of light brought into terrible distinctness the tumult that began to rage so suddenly within.

One hope only flashed into her brain—perhaps Raines was mistaken. But even then, if he were, Clayton must go some time; *he* had told her that. On this fact every thought became centred. It was no longer how he came, the richness of the new life he had shown her, the barrenness of the old, Raines's accusation, the shame of it—the shame of being pointed out and laughed at after Clayton's departure; it was no longer helpless wonder at the fierce emotions racking her for the first time: her whole being was absorbed in the realization which slowly forced itself into her heart and brain—some day he must go away; some day she must lose him. She lifted her hands to her head in a dazed, ineffectual way. The moonlight grew faint before her eyes; mountain, sky, and mist were indistinguishably blurred; and the girl sank down upon her trembling knees, down till she lay crouched on the floor with her tearless face in her arms.

The moon rose high above her and sank down the west. The shadows shortened and crept back to the woods, night noises grew fainter, and the mists floated up from the valley and clung around the mountain-tops; but she stirred only when a querulous voice came from within the cabin.

"Easter," it said, "ef Sherd Raines air gone, y'u better come in to bed. Y'u've got a lot o' work to do to-morrer."

The voice called her to the homely duties that had once filled her life and must fill it again. It was a summons to begin anew a life that was dead, and the girl lifted her haggard face in answer and rose wearily.

VII

ON the following Sunday morning, when
Clayton walked up to the cabin, Easter
and her mother were seated in the porch. He
called to them cheerily as he climbed over the
fence, but only the mother answered. Easter
rose as he approached, and, without speaking,
went within doors. He thought she must be ill,
so thin and drawn was her face, but her mother
said, carelessly:

"Oh, hit's only one o' Easter's spells.
She's been sort o' puny 'n' triflin' o' late, but
I reckon she'll be all right ag'in in a day or
two."

As the girl did not appear again, Clayton
concluded that she was lying down, and went
away without seeing her. Her manner had
seemed a little odd, but, attributing that to ill-
ness, he thought nothing further about it. To
his surprise, the incident was repeated, and
thereafter, to his wonder, the girl seemed to
avoid him. Their intimacy was broken sharply
off. When Clayton was at the cabin, either she
did not appear or else kept herself busied with

household duties. Their studies ceased abruptly. Easter had thrown her books into a corner,
her mother said, and did nothing but mope all
day; and though she insisted that it was only
one of the girl's "spells," it was plain that
something was wrong. Easter's face remained
thin and drawn, and acquired gradually a hard,
dogged, almost sullen look. She spoke to Clayton rarely, and then only in monosyllables. She
never looked him in the face, and if his gaze
rested intently on her, as she sat with eyes downcast and hands folded, she seemed to know it at
once. Her face would color faintly, her hands
fold and unfold nervously, and sometimes she
would rise and go within. He had no opportunity of speaking with her alone. She seemed
to guard against that, and, indeed, Raines's
presence almost prevented it, for the mountaineer was there always, and always now the last to
leave. He sat usually in the shadow of the vine,
and though his face was unseen, Clayton could
feel his eyes fixed upon him with an intensity
that sometimes made him nervous. The mountaineer had evidently begun to misinterpret his
visits to the cabin. Clayton was regarded as a
rival. In what other light, indeed, could he appear to Raines? Friendly calls between young
people of opposite sex were rare in the mountains. When a young man visited a young

woman, his intentions were supposed to be serious. Raines was plainly jealous.

But Easter? What was the reason for her odd behavior? Could she, too, have misconstrued his intentions as Raines had? It was impossible. But even if she had, his manner had in no wise changed. Some one else had aroused her suspicions, and if any one it must have been Raines. It was not the mother, he felt sure.

For some time Clayton's mother and sister had been urging him to make a visit home. He had asked leave of absence, but it was a busy time, and he had delayed indefinitely. In a fortnight, however, the stress of work would be over, and then he meant to leave. During that fortnight he was strangely troubled. He did not leave the camp, but his mind was busied with thoughts of Easter—nothing but Easter. Time and again he had reviewed their acquaintance minutely from the beginning, but he could find no cause for the change in her. When his work was done, he found himself climbing the mountain once more. He meant to solve the mystery if possible. He would tell Easter that he was going home. Surely she would betray some feeling then.

At the old fence which he had climbed so often he stopped, as was his custom, to rest a moment, with his eyes on the wild beauty before him—the great valley, with mists floating from its gloomy depths into the tremulous moonlight; far through the radiant space the still, dark masses of the Cumberland lifted in majesty against the east; and in the shadow of the great cliff the vague outlines of the old cabin, as still as the awful silence around it. A light was visible, but he could hear no voices. Still, he knew he would find the occupants seated in the porch, held by that strange quiet which nature imposes on those who dwell much alone with her. He had not been to the cabin for several weeks, and when he spoke Easter did not return his greeting; Raines nodded almost surlily, but from the mother came, as always, a cordial welcome.

"I'm mighty glad to see ye," she said; "you haven't been up fer a long time."

"No," answered Clayton; "I have been very busy—getting ready to go home." He had watched Easter closely as he spoke, but the girl did not lift her face, and she betrayed no emotion, not even surprise; nor did Raines. Only the mother showed genuine regret. The girl's apathy filled him with bitter disappointment. She had relapsed into barbarism again. He was a fool to think that in a few months he could counteract influences that had been moulding her character for a century. His purpose had been unselfish. Curiosity, the girl's beauty, his increasing power over her, had stimulated him, to be sure, but he had been conscientious and earnest. Somehow he was more than disappointed; he was hurt deeply, not only that he should have been so misunderstood, but for the lack of gratitude in the girl. He was bewildered. What could have happened? Could Raines really have poisoned her mind against him? Would Easter so easily believe what might have been said against him and not allow him a hearing?

" I've been expecting to take a trip home for several weeks," he found himself saying a moment later; " I think I shall go to-morrow."

He hardly meant what he said; a momentary pique had forced the words from him, but, once spoken, he determined to abide by them. Easter was stirred from her lethargy at last, but Clayton's attention was drawn to Raines's start of surprise, and he did not see the girl's face agitated for an instant, nor her hands nervously trembling in her lap.

"Ter-morrer!" cried the old woman. " Why, ye 'most take my breath away. I declar', I'm downright sorry you're goin', I hev tuk sech a shine to ye. I kind o' think I'll miss ye more'n Easter."

67

Raines's eyes turned to the girl, as did Clayton's. Not a suggestion of color disturbed the pallor of the girl's face, once more composed, and she said nothing.

"You're so jolly 'n' lively," continued the mother, 'n' ye allus hev so much to say. You air not like Easter 'n' Sherd hyar, who talk 'bout as much as two stumps. I suppose I'll hev to sit up 'n' talk to the moon when you air gone."

The mountaineer rose abruptly, and, though he spoke quietly, he could hardly control himself.

"Ez my company seems to be unwelcome to ye," he said, "I kin take it away from ye, 'n' I will."

Before the old woman could recover herself, he was gone.

"Well," she ejaculated, "whut kin be the matter with Sherd? He hev got mighty cur'us hyar of late, 'n' so hev Easter. All o' ye been a-settin' up hyar ez ef you was at a buryin'. I'm a-goin' to bed. You 'n' Easter kin set up long as ye please. I suppose you air comin' back ag'in to see us," she said, turning to Clayton.

"I don't know," he answered. "I may not; but I sha'n't forget you."

"Well, I wish ye good luck." Clayton shook hands with her, and she went within doors.

68

The girl had risen, too, with her mother, and was standing in the shadow.

" Good-by Easter," said Clayton, holding out his hand.

As she turned he caught one glimpse of her face in the moonlight, and its whiteness startled him. Her hand was cold when he took it, and her voice was scarcely audible as she faintly repeated his words. She lifted her face as their hands were unclasped, and her lips quivered mutely as if trying to speak, but he had turned to go. For a moment she watched his darkening figure, and then with stifled breath almost staggered into the cabin.

The road wound around the cliff and back again, and as Clayton picked his way along it he was oppressed by a strange uneasiness. Easter's face, as he last saw it, lay in his mind like a keen reproach. Could he have been mistaken? Had he been too hasty? He recalled the events of the evening. He began to see that it was significant that Raines had shown no surprise when he spoke of going home, and yet had seemed almost startled by the suddenness of his departure. Perhaps the mountaineer knew he was going. It was known at the camp. If he knew, then Easter must have known. Perhaps she had felt hurt because he had not spoken to her earlier. What might Raines not have told

69

her, and honestly, too? Perhaps he was unconsciously confirming all the mountaineer might have said. He ought to have spoken to her. Perhaps she could not speak to him. He wheeled suddenly in the path to return to the cabin, and stopped still.

Something was hurrying down through the undergrowth of the cliffside which towered darkly behind him. Nearer and nearer the bushes crackled as though some hunted animal were flying for life through them, and then through the laurel-hedge burst the figure of a woman, who sank to the ground in the path before him. The flash of yellow hair and a white face in the moonlight told him who it was.

"Easter, Easter!" he exclaimed, in sickening fear. "My God! is that you? Why, what is the matter, child? What are you doing here?"

He stooped above the sobbing girl, and pulled away her hands from her face, tear-stained and broken with pain. The limit of her self-repression was reached at last; the tense nerves, strained too much, had broken; and the passion, so long checked, surged through her like fire. Ah, God! what had he done? He saw the truth at last. In an impulse of tenderness he lifted the girl to her feet and held her, sobbing uncontrollably, in his arms, with her head against

70

his breast, and his cheek on her hair, soothing her as though she had been a child.

Presently she felt a kiss on her forehead. She looked up with a sudden fierce joy in her eyes, and their lips met.

VIII

CLAYTON shunned all self-questioning after that night. Stirred to the depths by that embrace on the mountain-side, he gave himself wholly up to the love or infatuation— he did not ask which—that enthralled him. Whatever it was, its growth had been subtle and swift. There was in it the thrill that might come from taming some wild creature that had never known control, and the gentleness that to any generous spirit such power would bring. These, with the magnetism of the girl's beauty and personality, and the influence of her environment, he had felt for a long time; but now richer chords were set vibrating in response to her great love, the struggle she had against its disclosure, the appeal for tenderness and protection in her final defeat. It was ideal, he told himself, as he sank into the delicious dream; they two alone with nature, above all human life, with its restraints, its hardships, its evils, its distress. For them was the freedom of the open sky lifting its dome above the mountains; for them nothing less kindly than the sun shining

72

its benediction; for their eyes only the changing
beauties of day and night; for their ears no sound
harsher than the dripping of dew or a bird-song;
for them youth, health, beauty, love.   And it
was primeval love, the love of the first woman
for the first man.   She knew no convention, no
prudery, no doubt.   Her life was impulse, and
her impulse was love.   She was the teacher
now, and he the taught; and he stood in wonder when the plant he had tended flowered into
such beauty in a single night.   Ah, the happy,
happy days that followed!   The veil that had
for a long time been unfolding itself between
him and his previous life seemed to have almost
fallen, and they were left alone to their happiness.   The mother kept her own counsel.
Raines had disappeared as though Death had
claimed him.   And the dream lasted till a summons home broke into it as the sudden flaring
up of a candle will shatter a reverie at twilight.

IX

THE summons was from his father, and was emphatic; and Clayton did not delay. The girl accepted his departure with a pale face, but with a quiet submission that touched him. Of Raines he had seen nothing and heard nothing since the night he had left the cabin in anger; but as he came down the mountain after bidding Easter good-by, he was startled by the mountaineer stepping from the bushes into the path.

"Ye air a-goin' home, I hear," he said, quietly.

"Yes," answered Clayton; "at midnight."

"Well, I'll walk down with ye a piece, ef ye don't mind. Hit's not out o' my way."

As he spoke his face was turned suddenly to the moonlight. The lines in it had sunk deeper, giving it almost an aged look; the eyes were hollow as from physical suffering or from fasting. He preceded Clayton down the path, with head bent, and saying nothing till they reached the spur of the mountain. Then in the same voice:

"I want to talk to ye awhile, 'n' I'd like to

hev ye step inter my house. I don't mean ye no harm," he added, quickly, " 'n' hit ain't fer."

"Certainly," said Clayton.

The mountaineer turned into the woods by a narrow path, and soon the outlines of a miserable little hut were visible through the dark woods. Raines thrust the door open. The single room was dark except for a few dull coals in a gloomy cavern which formed the fireplace.

"Sit down, ef ye kin find a cheer," said Raines. " 'n' I'll fix up the fire."

"Do you live here alone?" asked Clayton. He could hear the keen, smooth sound of the mountaineer's knife going through wood.

"Yes," he answered; " fer five year."

The coals brightened; tiny flames shot from them; in a moment the blaze caught the dry fagots, and shadows danced over the floor, wall, and ceiling, and vanished as the mountaineer rose from his knees. The room was as bare as the cell of a monk. A rough bed stood in one corner; a few utensils hung near the fireplace, wherein were remnants of potatoes roasting in the ashes, and close to the wooden shutter which served as a window was a board table. On it lay a large book—a Bible—a pen, a bottle of ink, and a piece of paper on which were letters traced with great care and difficulty. The mountaineer did not sit down, but began pacing the floor behind Clayton. Clayton moved his chair, and Raines seemed unconscious of his presence as with eyes on the floor he traversed the narrow width of the cabin.

"Y'u hevn't seed me up on the mount'in lately, hev ye?" he asked. "I reckon ye haven't missed me much. Do ye know whut I've been doin'?" he said, with sudden vehemence, stopping still and resting his eyes, which glowed like an animal's from the darkened end of the cabin, on Clayton.

"I've been tryin' to keep from killin' ye. Oh, don't move—don't fear now; ye air as safe as ef ye were down in the camp. I seed ye that night on the mount'in," he continued, pacing rapidly back and forth. "I was waitin' fer ye. I meant to tell ye jest whut I'm goin' to tell ye ter-night; 'n' when Easter come a-tearin' through the bushes, 'n' I seed ye—ye—a-standin' together "—the words seemed to stop in his throat—" I knowed I was too late.

"I sot thar fer a minute like a rock, 'n' when ye two went back up the mount'in, before I knowed it I was hyer in the house thar at the fire mouldin' a bullet to kill ye with as ye come back. All at oncet I heerd a voice plain as my own is at this minute:

"'Air you a-thinkin' 'bout takin' the life of

76

a fellow-creatur, Sherd Raines—*you* that air tryin' to be a servant o' the Lord?'

"But I kept on a-mouldin', 'n' suddenly I seed ye a-layin' in the road dead, 'n' the heavens opened 'n' the face o' the Lord was thar, 'n' he raised his hand to smite me with the brand o' Cain—'n' look thar!"

Clayton had sat spellbound by the terrible earnestness of the man, and as the mountaineer swept his dark hair back with one hand, he rose in sudden horror. Across the mountaineer's forehead ran a crimson scar yet unhealed. Could he have inflicted upon himself this fearful penance?

"Oh, it was only the moulds. I seed it all so plain that I throwed up my hands, fergittin' the moulds, 'n' the hot lead struck me thar; but," he continued, solemnly, "I knowed the Lord hed tuk that way o' punishin' me fer the sin o' havin' murder in my mind, 'n' I fell on my knees right thar a-prayin' fer fergiveness: 'n' since that night I hev stayed away from ye till the Lord give me power to stand ag'in the temptation o' harmin' ye. He hev showed me another way, 'n' now I hev come to ye as he hev tol' me. I hevn't tol' ye this fer nothin'. Y'u kin see now whut I think o' Easter, ef I was tempted to take the life o' the man who tuk her from me, 'n' I reckon ye will say I've got the

77

right to ax ye whut I'm a-goin' to. I hev knowed the gal sence she was a baby. We was children together, and thar hain't no use hidin' that I never keered a straw fer anuther woman. She used to be mighty wilful 'n' contrary, but as soon as you come I seed at oncet that a change was comin' over her. I mistrusted ye, 'n' I warned her ag'in' ye. But when I l'arned that ye was a-teachin' her, and a-doin' whut I had tried my best to do 'n' failed, I let things run along, thinkin' that mebbe ever'thing would come out right, after all. Mebbe hit *air* all right, but I come to ye now, 'n' I ax ye in the name of the livin' God, who is a-watchin' you 'n' a-guidin' me, air ye goin' to leave the po' gal to die sorrowin' fer ye, or do ye aim to come back 'n' marry her? "

Raines had stopped now in the centre of the cabin, and the shadows flickering slowly over him gave an unearthly aspect to his tall, gaunt figure, as he stood with uplifted arm, pale face, glowing eyes, and disordered hair.

"The gal hasn't got no protecter—her dad, as you know, is a-hidin' from jestice in the mount'ins—and I'm a-standin' in his place, 'n' I ax ye to do only whut you know ye ought."

There was nothing threatening in the mountaineer's attitude, nor dictatorial; and Clayton felt his right to say what he had, in spite of a natural impulse to resent such interference. Besides, there sprang up in his heart a sudden great admiration for this rough, uncouth fellow who was capable of such unselfishness; who, true to the trust of her father and his God, was putting aside the strongest passion of his life for what he believed was the happiness of the woman who had inspired it. He saw, too, that the sacrifice was made with perfect unconsciousness that it was unusual or admirable. He rose to his feet, and the two men faced each other.

"If you had told me this long ago," said Clayton, "I should have gone away, but you seemed distrustful and suspicious. I did not expect the present state of affairs to come about, but since it has, I tell you frankly that I have never thought of doing anything else than what you have asked."

And he told the truth, for he had already asked himself that question. Why should he not marry her? He must in all probability stay in the mountains for years, and after that time he would not be ashamed to take her home, so strong was his belief in her quickness and adaptability.

Raines seemed scarcely to believe what he heard. He had not expected such ready acquiescence. He had almost begun to fear from Clayton's silence that he was going to refuse, and then—God knows what he would have done.

Instantly he stretched out his hand.

" I hev done ye great wrong, 'n' I ax yer pardin," he said, huskily. " I want to say that I bear ye no gredge, 'n' thet I wish ye well. I hope ye won't think hard on me," he continued; " I hev had a hard fight with the devil as long as I can ricolect. I hev turned back time 'n' ag'in, but thar hain't nothin' ter keep me from goin' straight ahead now."

As Clayton left the cabin, the mountaineer stopped him for a moment on the threshold.

" Thar's another thing I reckon I ought to tell ye," he said; " Easter's dad air powerfully sot ag'in ye. He thought ye was an officer at fust, 'n' hit was hard to git him out o' the idee thet ye was spyin' fer him; 'n' when he seed ye goin' to the house, he got it inter his head that ye mought be meanin' harm to Easter, who air the only thing alive thet he keers fer much. He promised not to tech ye, 'n' I knowed he would keep his word as long as he was sober. It'll be all right now, I reckon," he concluded, " when I tell him whut ye aims to do, though he hev got a spite ag'in all furriners. Far'well! I wish ye well; I wish ye well."

An hour later Clayton was in Jellico. It was midnight when the train came in, and he went immediately to his berth. Striking the curtain accidentally, he loosed it from its fastenings, and, doubling the pillows, he lay looking out on the swiftly passing landscape. The moon was full and brilliant, and there was a strange, keen pleasure in being whirled in such comfort through the night. The mists almost hid the mountains. They seemed very, very far away. A red star trembled in the crest of Wolf Mountain. Easter's cabin must be almost under that star. He wondered if she were asleep. Perhaps she was out on the porch, lonely, suffering, and thinking of him. He felt her kiss and her tears upon his hand. Did he not love her? Could there be any doubt about that? His thoughts turned to Raines, and he saw the mountaineer in his lonely cabin, sitting with his head bowed in his hands in front of the dying fire. He closed his eyes, and another picture rose before him—a scene at home. He had taken Easter to New York. How brilliant the light! what warmth and luxury! There stood his father, there his mother. What gracious dignity they had! Here was his sister—what beauty and elegance and grace of manner! But Easter! Wherever she was placed the other figures needed readjustment. There was something irritably incongruous—Ah! now he had it—his mind grew hazy—he was asleep.

X

DURING the weeks that followed, some malignant spirit seemed to be torturing him with a slow realization of all he had lost; taunting him with the possibility of regaining it and the certainty of losing it forever.

As he stepped from the dock at Jersey City the fresh sea wind had thrilled him like a memory, and his pulses leaped instantly into sympathy with the tense life that vibrated in the air. He seemed never to have been away so long, and never had home seemed so pleasant. His sister had grown more beautiful; his mother's quiet, noble face was smoother and fairer than it had been for years; and despite the absence of his father, who had been hastily summoned to England, there was an air of cheerfulness in the house that was in marked contrast to its gloom when Clayton was last at home. He had been quickened at once into a new appreciation of the luxury and refinement about him, and he soon began to wonder how he had inured himself to the discomforts and crudities of his mountain life. Old habits easily resumed sway over him. At the club friend and acquaintance were so unfeignedly glad to see him that he began to suspect that his own inner gloom had darkened their faces after his father's misfortune. Day after day found him in his favorite corner at the club, watching the passing pageant and listening eagerly to the conversational froth of the town—the gossip of club, theatre, and society. His ascetic life in the mountains gave to every pleasure the taste of inexperience. His early youth seemed renewed, so keen and fresh were his emotions. He felt, too, that he was recovering a lost identity, and still the new one that had grown around him would not loosen its hold. He had told his family nothing of Easter—why, he could scarcely have said—and the difficulty of telling increased each day. His secret began to weigh heavily upon him; and though he determined to unburden himself on his father's return, he was troubled with a vague sense of deception. When he went to receptions with his sister, this sense of a double identity was keenly felt amid the lights, the music, the flowers, the flash of eyes and white necks and arms, the low voices, the polite, clearcut utterances of welcome and compliment.

Several times he had met a face for which he had once had a boyish infatuation. Its image had never been supplanted during his student

career, but he had turned from it as from a star
when he came home and found that his life was
to be built with his own hands. Now the girl
had grown to gracious womanhood, and when
he saw her he was thrilled with the remembrance
that she had once favored him above all others.
One night a desire assailed him to learn upon
what footing he then stood. He had yielded,
and she gave him a kindly welcome. They had
drifted to reminiscence, and Clayton went home
that night troubled at heart and angry that he
should be so easily disturbed; surprised that the
days were passing so swiftly, and pained that
they were filled less and less with thoughts of
Easter. With a pang of remorse and fear, he
determined to go back to the mountains as soon
as his father came home. He knew the effect
of habit. He would forget these pleasures felt
so keenly now, as he had once forgotten them,
and he would leave before their hold upon him
was secure.

Knowing the danger that beset him, Puritan
that he was, he had avoided it all he could. He
even stopped his daily visits to the club, and
spent most of his time at home with his mother
and sister. Once only, to his bitter regret, was
he induced to go out. Wagner's tidal wave had
reached New York; it was the opening night of
the season, and the opera was one that he had

learned to love in Germany. The very bril-
liancy of the scene threw him into gloom, so
aloof did he feel from it all—the great theatre
aflame with lights, the circling tiers of faces, the
pit with its hundred musicians, their eyes on the
leader, who stood above them with baton up-
raised and German face already aglow.

In his student days he had loved music, but
he had little more than trifled with it; now,
strangely enough, his love, even his understanding, seemed to have grown; and when the
violins thrilled all the vast space into life,
he was shaken with a passion newly born.
All the evening he sat riveted. A rush of
memories came upon him—memories of his
student life, with its dreams and ideals of cul-
ture and scholarship, which rose from his past
again like phantoms. In the elevation of the
moment the trivial pleasures that had been
tempting him became mean and unworthy.
With a pang of bitter regret he saw himself as
he might have been, as he yet might be.

A few days later his father came home, and
his distress of mind was complete. Clayton
need stay in the mountains but little longer, he
said; he was fast making up his losses, and he
had hoped after his trip to England to have
Clayton at once in New York; but now he had
best wait perhaps another year. Then had

come a struggle that racked heart and brain. All he had ever had was before him again. Could it be his duty to shut himself from this life—his natural heritage—to stifle the highest demands of his nature? Was he seriously in love with that mountain girl? Had he indeed ever been sure of himself? If, then, he did not love her beyond all question, would he not wrong himself, wrong her, by marrying her? Ah, but might he not wrong her, wrong himself —even more? He was bound to her by every tie that his sensitive honor recognized among the duties of one human being to another. He had sought her; he had lifted her above her own life. If one human being had ever put its happiness in the hands of another, that had been done. If he had not deliberately taught her to love him, he had not tried to prevent it. He could not excuse himself; the thought of gaining her affection had occurred to him, and he had put it aside. There was no excuse; for when she gave her love, he had accepted it, and, as far as she knew, had given his own unreservedly. Ah, that fatal moment of weakness, that night on the mountain-side! Could he tell her, could he tell Raines, the truth, and ask to be released? What could Easter with her devotion, and Raines with his singleness of heart, know of this substitute for love which civilization had taught him? Or, granting that they could understand, he might return home; but Easter—what was left for her?

It was useless to try to persuade himself that her love would fade away, perhaps quickly, and leave no scar; that Raines would in time win her for himself, his first idea of their union be realized, and, in the end, all happen for the best. That might easily be possible with a different nature under different conditions—a nature less passionate, in contact with the world and responsive to varied interests; but not with Easter—alone with a love that had shamed him, with mountain, earth, and sky unchanged, and the vacant days marked only by a dreary round of wearisome tasks. He remembered Raines's last words—" Air ye goin' to leave the po' gal to die sorrowin' fer ye? " What happiness would be possible for him with that lonely mountain-top and the white, drawn face forever haunting him?

That very night a letter came, with a rude superscription—the first from Easter. Within it was a poor tintype, from which Easter's eyes looked shyly at him. Before he left he had tried in vain to get her to the tent of an itinerant photographer. During his absence, she had evidently gone of her own accord. The face was very beautiful, and in it was an expression of questioning, modest pride. "Aren't you surprised? " it seemed to say—" and pleased? " Only the face, with its delicate lines, and the throat and the shoulders were visible. She looked almost refined. And the note—it was badly spelled and written with great difficulty, but it touched him. She was lonely, she said, and she wanted him to come back. Lonely— that cry was in each line.

His response to this was an instant resolution to go back at once, and, sensitive and pliant as his nature was, there was no hesitation for him when his duty was clear and a decision once made. With great care and perfect frankness he had traced the history of his infatuation in a letter to his father, to be communicated when the latter chose to his mother and sister. Now he was nearing the mountains again.

XI

THE journey to the mountains was made with a heavy heart. In his absence everything seemed to have suffered a change. Jellico had never seemed so small, so coarse, so wretched as when he stepped from the dusty train and saw it lying dwarfed and shapeless in the afternoon sunlight. The State line bisects the straggling streets of frame-houses. On the Kentucky side an extraordinary spasm of morality had quieted into local option. Just across the way in Tennessee was a row of saloons. It was "pay-day" for the miners, and the worst element of all the mines was drifting in to spend the following Sabbath in unchecked vice. Several rough, brawny fellows were already staggering from Tennessee into Kentucky, and around one saloon hung a crowd of slatternly negroes, men and women. Heartsick with disgust, Clayton hurried into the lane that wound through the valley. Were these hovels, he asked himself in wonder, the cabins he once thought so poetic, so picturesque? How was it that they suggested now only a pitiable poverty of life? From each, as he passed, came a rough, cordial shout of greeting. Why was he jarred so strangely? Even nature had changed. The mountains seemed stunted, less beautiful. The light, streaming through the western gap with all the splendor of a mountain sunset, no longer thrilled him. The moist fragrance of the earth at twilight, the sad pipings of birds by the way-side, the faint, clear notes of a wood-thrush—his favorite—from the edge of the forest, even the mid-air song of a meadow-lark above his head, were unheeded as, with face haggard with thought and travel, he turned doggedly from the road and up the mountain toward Easter's home. The novelty and ethnological zeal that had blinded him to the disagreeable phases of mountain life were gone; so was the pedestal from which he had descended to make a closer study of the people. For he felt now that he had gone among them with an unconscious con-descension; his interest seemed now to have been little more than curiosity—a pastime to escape brooding over his own change of fortune. And with Easter—ah, how painfully clear his mental vision had grown! Was it the tragedy of wast-ing possibilities that had drawn him to her—to help her—or was it his own miserable selfish-ness, after all?

No one was visible when he reached the

cabin. The calm of mountain and sky enthralled it as completely as the cliff that towered behind it. The day still lingered, and the sunlight rested lightly on each neighboring crest. As he stepped upon the porch there was a slight noise within the cabin, and, peering into the dark interior, he called Easter's name. There was no answer, and he sank wearily into a chair, his thoughts reverting homeward. By this time his mother and sister must know why he had come back to the mountains. He could imagine their consternation and grief. Perhaps that was only the beginning; he might be on the eve of causing them endless unhappiness. He had thought to involve them as little as possible by remaining in the mountains; but the thought of living there was now intolerable in the new relations he would sustain to the people. What should he do? where go? As he bent forward in perplexity, there was a noise again in the cabin—this time the stealthy tread of feet—and before he could turn, a rough voice vibrated threateningly in his ears:

"Say who ye air, and what yer business is, mighty quick, er ye hain't got a minute to live."

Clayton looked up, and to his horror saw the muzzle of a rifle pointed straight at his head. At the other end of it, and standing in the door, was a short, stocky figure, a head of bushy hair, and a pair of small, crafty eyes. The fierceness and suddenness of the voice, in the great silence about him, and its terrible earnestness, left him almost paralyzed.

"Come, who air ye? Say quick, and don't move, nother."

Clayton spoke his name with difficulty. The butt of the rifle dropped to the floor, and with a harsh laugh its holder advanced to him with hand outstretched:

"So ye air Easter's feller, air ye? Well, I'm yer dad—that's to be. Shake."

Clayton shuddered. Good heavens! this was Easter's father! More than once or twice, his name had never been mentioned at the cabin.

"I tuk ye fer a raider," continued the old mountaineer, not noticing Clayton's repulsion, "'n' ef ye had 'a' been, ye wouldn't be nobody now. I reckon Easter hain't told ye much about me, 'n' I reckon she hev a right to be a leetle ashamed of me. I had a leetle trouble down thar in the valley—I s'pose you've heerd about it—'n' I've had to keep kind o' quiet. I seed ye once afore, 'n' I come near shootin' ye, thinkin' ye was a raider. Am mighty glad I didn't, fer Easter is powerful sot on ye. Sherd thought I could resk comin' down to the weddin'. They hev kind o' give up the s'arch, 'n' none o' the boys won't tell on me. We'll have

an old-timer, I tell ye. Ye folks from the settlemints air mighty high-heeled, but old Bill Hicks
don't allus go bar'footed. He kin step purty
high, 'n' he's a-goin' to do it at that weddin'.
Hev somefin?" he asked, suddenly pulling out
a flask of colorless liquid. "Ez ye air to be one
o' the fambly, I don't mind tellin' ye thar's the
very moonshine that caused the leetle trouble
down in the valley."

For fear of giving offence, Clayton took a
swallow of the liquid, which burned him like
fire. He had scarcely recovered from the first
shock, and he had listened to the man and
watched him with a sort of enthralling fascina-
tion. He was Easter's father. He could even
see a faint suggestion of Easter's face in the cast
of the features before him, coarse and degraded
as they were. He had the same nervous, im-
petuous quickness, and, horrified by the likeness,
Clayton watched him sink back into a chair, pipe
in mouth, and relapse into a stolidity that
seemed incapable of the energy and fire shown
scarcely a moment before. His life in the
mountains had made him as shaggy as some
wild animal. He was coatless, and his trousers
of jeans were upheld by a single home-made
suspender. His beard was yet scarcely touched
with gray, and his black, lustreless hair fell from
under a round hat of felt with ragged edges and

93

uncertain color. The mountaineer did not speak again until, with great deliberation and care, he had filled a cob pipe. Then he bent his sharp eyes upon Clayton so fixedly that the latter let his own fall.

"Mebbe ye don't know that I'm ag'in' furriners," he said, abruptly, " all o' ye; 'n' ef the Lord hisself hed 'a' tol' me thet my gal would be a-marryin' one, I wouldn't 'a' believed him. But Sherd hev told me ye air all right, 'n' ef Sherd says ye air, why, ye air, I reckon, 'n' I hevn't got nothin' to say; though I hev got a heap ag'in ye—all o' ye."

His voice had a hint of growing anger under the momentary sense of his wrongs, and, not wishing to incense him further, Clayton said nothing.

"Ye air back a little sooner than ye expected, ain't ye?" he asked, presently, with an awkward effort at good-humor. " I reckon ye air gittin' anxious. Well, we hev been gittin' ready fer ye, 'n' you 'n' Easter kin hitch ez soon ez ye please. Sherd Raines air goin' to do the marryin'. He air the best friend I got. Sherd was a-courtin' the gal, too, but he hevn't got no gredge ag'in ye, 'n' he hev promised to tie ye. Sherd air a preacher now. He hev just got his license. He didn't want to do it, but I told him he had to. We'll hev the biggest wed-

din' ever seed in these mountains, I tell ye. Any
o' yo' folks be on hand?"

"No," answered Clayton, soberly, "I think
not."

"Well, I reckon we kin fill up the house."

Clayton's heart sank at the ordeal of a wedding with such a master of ceremonies. He was
about to ask where Easter and her mother were,
when, to his relief, he saw them both in the
path below, approaching the house. The girl
was carrying a bucket of water on her head.
Once he would have thought her picturesque,
but now it pained him to see her doing such
rough work. When she saw him, she gave a
cry of surprise and delight that made Clayton
tingle with remorse. Then running to him with
glowing face, she stopped suddenly, and, with
a look down at her bare feet and soiled gown,
fled into the cabin. Clayton followed, but the
room was so dark he could see nothing.

"Easter!" he called. There was no answer,
but he was suddenly seized about the neck by
a pair of unseen arms and kissed by unseen lips
twice in fierce succession, and before he could
turn and clasp the girl she was laughing softly
in the next room, with a barred door between
them. Clayton waited patiently several minutes, and then asked:

"Easter, aren't you ready?"

95

"Not yit—not *yet!*" She corrected herself with such vehemence that Clayton laughed. She came out presently, and blushed when Clayton looked her over from head to foot with astonishment. She was simply and prettily dressed in white muslin; a blue ribbon was about her throat, and her hair was gathered in a Psyche knot that accented the classicism of her profile. Her appearance was really refined and tasteful. When they went out on the porch he noticed that her hands had lost their tanned appearance. Her feet were slippered, and she wore black stockings. He remembered the book of fashion-plates he had once sent her; it was that that had quickened her instinct of dress. He said nothing, but the happy light in Easter's face shone brighter as she noted his pleased and puzzled gaze.

"Why, ye look like another man," said Easter's mother, who had been looking Clayton over with a quizzical smile. "Is that the way folks dress out in the settlemints? 'N' look at that gal. Ef she hev done anythin' sence ye hev been gone but——" The rest of the sentence was smothered in the palm of Easter's hand, and she too began scrutinizing Clayton closely. The mountaineer said nothing, and after a curious glance at Easter resumed his pipe.

96

" You look like a pair of butterflies," said the mother when released. "Sherd oughter be mighty proud of his first marryin'. I s'pose ye know he air a preacher now? Ye oughter heerd him preach last Sunday. It was his fust time. The way he lighted inter the furriners was a caution. He 'lowed he was a-goin' to fight cyard-playin' and dancin' ez long ez he hed breath."

"Yes; 'n' thar's whar Sherd air a fool. I'm ag'in furriners, too, but thar hain't no harm in dancin', 'n' thar's goin' to be dancin' at this weddin' ef I'm alive."

Easter shrank perceptibly when her father spoke, and looked furtively at Clayton, who winced, in spite of himself, as the rough voice grated in his ear. Instantly her face grew unhappy, and contained an appeal for pardon that he was quick to understand and appreciate. Thereafter he concealed his repulsion, and treated the rough bear so affably that Easter's eyes grew moist with gratitude.

Darkness was gathering in the valley below when he rose to go. Easter had scarcely spoken to him, but her face and her eyes, fixed always upon him, were eloquent with joy. Once as she passed behind him her hand rested with a timid, caressing touch upon his shoulder, and now, as he walked away from the porch, she called him back. He turned, and she had gone into the house.

" What is it, Easter? " he asked, stepping into the dark room. His hand was grasped in both her own and held tremblingly.

" Don't mind dad," she whispered, softly. Something warm and moist fell upon his hand as she unloosed it, and she was gone.

That night he wrote home in a better frame of mind. The charm of the girl's personality had asserted its power again, and hopes that had almost been destroyed by his trip home were rekindled by her tasteful appearance, her delicacy of feeling, and by her beauty, which he had not overrated. He asked that his sister might meet him in Louisville after the wedding— whenever that should be. They two could decide then what should be done. His own idea was to travel; and so great was his confidence in Easter, he believed that, in time, he could take her to New York without fear.

XII

IT was plain that Raines—to quiet the old
man's uneasiness, perhaps—had told him
of his last meeting with Clayton, and that, during the absence of the latter, some arrangements
for the wedding had been made, even by Easter,
who in her trusting innocence had perhaps never
thought of any other end to their relations. In
consequence, there was an unprecedented stir
among the mountaineers. The marriage of a
" citizen " with a " furriner " was an unprecedented event, and the old mountaineer, who began to take some pride in the alliance, empha-
sized it at every opportunity.

At the mines Clayton's constant visits to the
mountain were known to everybody, but little
attention had been paid to them. Now, however, when the rumor of the wedding seemed
confirmed by his return and his silence, every
one was alert with a curiosity so frankly shown
that he soon became eager to get away from the
mountains. Accordingly, he made known his
wish to Easter's parents that the marriage
should take place as soon as possible. Both re-

ceived the suggestion with silent assent. Then had followed many difficulties. Only as a great concession to the ideas and customs of "furriners" would the self-willed old mountaineer agree that the ceremony should take place at night, and that after the supper and the dance, the two should leave Jellico at daybreak. Mountain marriages were solemnized in the daytime, and wedding journeys were unknown. The old man did not understand why Clayton should wish to leave the mountains, and the haste of the latter seemed to give him great offence. When Clayton had ventured to suggest, instead, that the marriage should be quiet, and that he and Easter should remain on the mountain a few days before leaving, he fumed with anger; and thereafter any suggestion from the young engineer was met with a suspicion that looked ominous. Raines was away on his circuit, and would not return until just before the wedding, so that from him Clayton could get no help. Very wisely, then, he interfered no more, but awaited the day with dread.

It was nearing dusk when he left the camp on his wedding-night. Half-way up the mountain he stopped to lean against the kindly breast of a bowlder blocking the path. It was the spot where he had seen Easter for the first time. The mountains were green again, as they were then, but the scene seemed sadly changed. The sun was gone; the evening-star had swung its white light like a censer above Devil's Den; the clouds were moving swiftly through the darkening air, like a frightened flock seeking a fold; and the night was closing fast over the cluster of faint camp-fires. The spirit brooding over mountain and sky was unspeakably sad, and with a sharp pain at his heart Clayton turned from it and hurried on. Mountain, sky, and valley were soon lost in the night. When he reached the cabin rays of bright light were flashing from chink and crevice into the darkness, and from the kitchen came the sounds of busy preparation. Already many guests had arrived. A group of men who stood lazily talking in the porch became silent as he approached, but, recognizing none of them, he entered the cabin. A dozen women were seated about the room, and instantly their eyes were glued upon him. As the kitchen door swung open he saw Easter's mother bending over the fireplace, a table already heavily laden, and several women bustling about it. Above his head he heard laughter, a hurried tramping of feet, and occasional cries of surprise and delight. He paused at the threshold, hardly knowing what to do, and when he turned a titter from one corner showed that his embarrassment was seen. On the porch he was seized by Easter's father, who drew him back into the room. The old mountaineer's face was flushed, and he had been drinking heavily.

"Oh, hyar ye air!" he exclaimed. "You're right on hand, hain't ye? Hyar, Bill," he called, thrusting his head out of the door, "you 'n' Jim 'n' Milt come in hyar." Three awkward young mountaineers entered. "These fellers air goin' to help ye."

They were to be his ushers. Clayton shook hands with them gravely.

"Oh, we air about ready fer ye, 'n' we air only waitin' fer Sherd and the folks to come," continued the mountaineer, jubilantly, winking significantly at Clayton and his attendants, who stood about him at the fireplace. Clayton shook his head firmly, but the rest followed Hicks, who turned at the door and repeated the invitation with a frowning face. Clayton was left the focus of feminine eyes, whose unwavering directness kept his own gaze on the floor. People began to come in rapidly, most of whom he had never seen before. The room was filled, save for a space about him. Every one gave him a look of curiosity that made him feel like some strange animal on exhibition. Once more he tried to escape to the porch, and again he was met by Easter's father, who this time was accompanied by Raines.

The young circuit-rider was smoothly shaven, and dressed in dark clothes, and his calm face and simple but impressive manner seemed at once to alter the atmosphere of the room. He grasped Clayton's hand warmly, and without a trace of self-consciousness. The room had grown instantly quiet, and Raines began to share the curious interest that Clayton had caused; for the young mountaineer's sermon had provoked discussion far and wide, and, moreover, the peculiar relations of the two toward Easter were known and rudely appreciated. Hicks was subdued into quiet respect, and tried to conceal his incipient intoxication. The effort did not last long. When the two fiddlers came, he led them in with a defiant air, and placed them in the corner, bustling about officiously but without looking at Raines, whose face began to cloud.

"Well, we're all hyar, I reckon!" he exclaimed, in his terrible voice. "Is Easter ready?" he shouted up the steps.

A confused chorus answered him affirmatively, and he immediately arranged Clayton in one corner of the room with his serious attendants on one side, and Raines, grave to solemnity, on the other. Easter's mother and her assistants came in from the kitchen, and the doors were filled with faces. Above, the tramping of feet became more hurried; below, all stood with expectant faces turned to the rude staircase. Clayton's heart began to throb, and a strange light brightened under Raines's heavy brows.

"Hurry up, thar!" shouted Hicks, impatiently.

A moment later two pairs of rough shoes came down the steps, and after them two slippered feet that fixed every eye in the room, until the figure and face above them slowly descended into the light. Midway the girl paused with a timid air. Had an angel been lowered to mortal view, the waiting people would not have been stricken with more wonder. Raines's face relaxed into a look almost of awe, and even Hicks for the instant was stunned into reverence. Mountain eyes had never beheld such loveliness so arrayed. It was simple enough—the garment—all white, and of a misty texture, yet it formed a mysterious vision to them. About the girl's brow was a wreath of pink and white laurel. A veil had not been used. It would hide her face, she said, and she did not see why that should be done. For an instant she stood poised so lightly that she seemed to sway like a vision, as the candle-lights quivered about her, with her hands clasped in front of her, and her eyes wandering about the room till

they lighted upon Clayton with a look of love
that seemed to make her conscious only of him.
Then, with quickening breath, lips parted slightly, cheeks slowly flushing, and shining eyes still
upon him, she moved slowly across the room
until she stood at his side.

Raines gathered himself together as from a
dream, and stepped before the pair. Broken and
husky at first, his voice trembled in spite of himself, but thereafter there was no hint of the
powerful emotions at play within him. Only as
he joined their hands, his eyes rested an instant
with infinite tenderness on Easter's face—as
though the look were a last farewell—and his
voice deepened with solemn earnestness when
he bade Clayton protect and cherish her until
death. There was a strange mixture in those
last words of the office and the man—of di-
vine authority and personal appeal—and Clayton was deeply stirred. The benediction over,
the young preacher was turning away, when
some one called huskily from the rear of the
cabin:

" Whyn't ye kiss the bride? "

It was Easter's father, and the voice, rough
as it was, brought a sensation of relief to all.
The young mountaineer's features contracted
with swift pain, and as Easter leaned toward
him, with subtle delicacy, he touched, not her

lips, but her forehead, as reverently as though she had been a saint.

Instantly the fiddles began, the floor was cleared, the bridal party hurried into the kitchen, and the cabin began to shake beneath dancing feet. Hicks was fulfilling his word, and in the kitchen his wife had done her part. Everything known to the mountaineer palate was piled in profusion on the table, but Clayton and Easter ate nothing. To him the whole evening was a nightmare, which the solemn moments of the marriage had made the more hideous. He was restless and eager to get away. The dancing was becoming more furious, and above the noise rose Hicks's voice prompting the dancers. The ruder ones still hung about the doors, regarding Clayton curiously, or with eager eyes upon the feast. Easter was vaguely troubled, and conflicting with the innocent pride and joy in her eyes were the questioning glances she turned to Clayton's darkening face. At last they were hurried out, and in came the crowd like hungry wolves.

Placing Clayton and Easter in a corner of the room, the attendants themselves took part in the dancing, and such dancing Clayton had never seen. Doors and windows were full of faces, and the room was crowded; from the kitchen came coarse laughter and the rattling of dishes.

Occasionally Hicks would disappear with several others, and would return with his face redder than ever.

Easter became uneasy. Once she left Clayton's side and expostulated with her father, but he shook her from his arm roughly. Raines saw this, and a moment later he led the old mountaineer from the room. Thereafter the latter was quieter, but only for a little while. Several times the kitchen was filled and emptied, and ever was the crowd unsteadier. Soon even Raines's influence was of no avail, and the bottle was passed openly from guest to guest.

"Whyn't ye dance?"

Clayton felt his arm grasped, and Hicks stood swaying before him.

"Whyn't ye dance?" he repeated. "Can't ye dance? Mebbe ye air too good—like Sherd. Well, Easter kin. Hyar, Mart, come 'n' dance with the gal. She air the best dancer in these parts."

Clayton had his hand upon Easter as though to forbid her. The mountaineer saw the movement, and his face flamed; but before he could speak, the girl pressed Clayton's arm, and, with an appealing glance, rose to her feet.

"That's right," said her father, approvingly, but with a look of drunken malignancy toward Clayton. "Now," he called out, in a loud voice, " I want this couple to have the floor, 'n' everybody to look on 'n' see what is dancin'. Start the fiddles, boys."

It was dancing. The young mountaineer was a slender, active fellow, not without grace, and Easter seemed hardly to touch the floor. They began very slowly at first, till Easter, glancing aside at Clayton and seeing his face deepen with interest, and urged by the remonstrance of her father, the remarks of the onlookers, and the increasing abandon of the music, gave herself up to the dance. The young mountaineer was no mean partner. Forward and back they glided, their swift feet beating every note of the music; Easter receding before her partner, and now advancing toward him, now whirling away with a disdainful toss of her head and arms, and now giving him her hand and whirling till her white skirts floated from the floor. At last, with head bent coquettishly toward her partner, she danced around him, and when it seemed that she would be caught by his out-stretched hands she slipped from his clasp, and, with burning cheeks, flashing eyes, and bridal wreath showering its pink-flecked petals about her, flew to Clayton's side.

" Mebbe ye don't like that," cried Hicks, turning to Raines, who had been gravely watching the scene.

Raines said nothing in reply, but only looked the drunken man in the face.

" You two," he continued, indicating Clayton with an angry shake of his head, " air a-tryin' to spile ever'body's fun. Both of ye air too high-heeled fer us folks. Y'u hev got mighty good now that ye air a preacher," he added, with a drunken sneer, irritated beyond endurance by Raines's silence and his steady look. " I want ye to know Bill Hicks air a-runnin' things here, 'n' I don't want no meddlin'. I'll drink right here in front o' ye "—holding a bottle defiantly above his head—" 'n' I mean to dance, too, I warn ye now," he added, staggering toward the door, " I don't want no meddlin'."

Easter had buried her face in her hands. Her mother stood near her husband, helplessly trying to get him away, and fearing to arouse him more. Raines was the most composed man in the room, and a few moments later, when dancing was resumed, Clayton heard his voice at his ear:

" You'd better go upstairs 'n' wait till it's time to go," he said. " He hev got roused ag'in ye, and ag'in me too. I'll keep out o' his way so as not to aggravate him, but I'll stay hyar fer fear something will happen. Mebbe he'll sober up a little, but I'm afeard he'll drink more'n ever."

A moment later, unseen by the rest, the two mounted the stairway to the little room where Easter's girlhood had been passed. To Clayton the peace of the primitive little chamber was an infinite relief. A dim light showed a rude bed in one corner and a pine table close by, whereon lay a few books and a pen and an ink-bottle. Above, the roof rose to a sharp angle, and the low, unplastered walls were covered with pictures cut from the books he had given her. A single window opened into the night over the valley and to the mountains beyond. Two small cane-bottom chairs were near this, and in these they sat down. In the east dark clouds were moving swiftly across the face of the moon, checking its light and giving the dim valley startling depth and blackness. Rain-drops struck the roof at intervals, a shower of apple-blossoms rustled against the window and drifted on, and below the muffled sound of music and shuffling feet was now and then pierced by the shrill calls of the prompter. There was something ominous in the persistent tread of feet and the steady flight of the gloomy clouds, and quivering with vague fears, Easter sank down from her chair to Clayton's feet, and burst into tears, as he put his arms tenderly about her.

" Has he ever treated you badly ? "

"No, no," she answered; "it's only the whiskey."

It was not alone of her father's behavior that she was thinking. Memories were busy within her, and a thousand threads of feeling were tightening her love of home, the only home she had ever known. Now she was leaving it for a strange world of which she knew nothing, and the thought pierced her like a physical pain.

"Are we ever coming back ag'in?" she asked, with sudden fear.

"Yes, dear," answered Clayton, divining her thoughts; "whenever you wish."

After that she grew calmer, and remained quiet so long that she seemed to have fallen asleep like a tired child relieved of its fears. Leaning forward, he looked into the darkness. It was after midnight, surely. The clouds had become lighter, more luminous, and gradually the moon broke through them, lifting the pall from the valley, playing about the edge of the forest, and quivering at last on the window. As he bent back to look at the sleeping girl, the moonlight fell softly upon her face, revealing its purity of color, and touching the loosened folds of her hair, and shining through a tear-drop which had escaped from her closed lashes. How lovely the face was! How pure! How child-

like with all its hidden strength! How absolute her confidence in him! How great her love!
It was of her love that he thought, not of his
own; but with a new realization of her depend-
ence upon him for happiness, his clasp tightened
about her almost unconsciously. She stirred
slightly, and, bending his head lower, Clayton
whispered in her ear:

" Have you been asleep, dear? "

She lifted her face and looked tenderly into
his eyes, shaking her head slowly, and then, as
he bent over again, she clasped her arms about
his neck and strained his face to hers.

Not until the opening of the door at the stairway stirred them did they notice that the music
and dancing below had ceased. The door was
instantly closed again after a slight sound of
scuffling, and in the moment of stillness that
followed, they heard Raines say calmly:

" No; you can't go up thar."

A brutal oath answered him, and Easter
started to her feet when she heard her father's
voice, terrible with passion; but Clayton held
her back, and hurried down the stairway.

" Ef ye don't come away from that door,"
he could hear Hicks saying, " 'n' stop this meddlin', I'll kill you 'stid o' the furriner."

As Clayton thrust the door open, Raines was
standing a few feet from the stairway. The

drunken man was struggling in the grasp of
several mountaineers, who were coaxing and
dragging him across the room. About them
were several other men scarcely able to stand,
and behind these a crowd of shrinking women.

"Git back! git back!" said Raines, in low,
hurried tones.

But Hicks had caught sight of Clayton. For
a moment he stood still, glaring at him. Then,
with a furious effort, he wrenched himself from
the men who held him, and thrust his hand into
his pocket, backing against the wall. The crowd
fell away from him as a weapon was drawn and
levelled with unsteady hand at Clayton. Raines
sprang forward; Clayton felt his arm clutched,
and a figure darted past him. The flash came,
and when Raines wrenched the weapon from the
mountaineer's grasp the latter was standing
rigid, with horror-stricken eyes fixed upon the
smoke, in which Easter's white face showed like
an apparition. As the smoke drifted aside,
the girl was seen with both hands at her
breast. Then, while a silent terror held every
one, she turned, and, with outstretched hands,
tottered toward Clayton; and as he caught
her in his arms, a low moan broke from her
lips.

Some one hurried away for a physician, but
the death-watch was over before he came.

For a long time the wounded girl lay apparently unconscious, her face white and quiet.
Only when a wood-thrush called from the woods
close by were her lids half raised, and as Clayton pushed the shutter open above her and lifted
her gently, she opened her eyes with a grate-
ful look and turned her face eagerly to the
cool air.

The dawn was breaking. The east was already aflame with bars of rosy light, gradually
widening. Above them a single star was poised,
and in the valley below great white mists were
stirring from sleep. For a moment she seemed
to be listlessly watching the white, shapeless
things, trembling as with life, and creeping
silently into wood and up glen; and then her
lashes drooped wearily together.

The door opened as Clayton let her sink upon
the bed, breathing as if asleep, and he turned,
expecting the physician. Raines, too, rose
eagerly, stopped suddenly, and shrank back with
a shudder of repulsion as the figure of the
wretched father crept, half crouching, within.

" Sherd ! "

The girl's tone was full of gentle reproach,
and so soft that it reached only Clayton's ears.

" Sherd ! "

This time his name was uttered with an appeal ever so gentle.

"Pore dad! Pore dad!" she whispered. Her clasp tightened suddenly on Clayton's hand, and her eyes were held to his, even while the light in them was going out.

A week later two men left the cabin at dusk. Half-way down the slope they came to one of the unspeakably mournful little burying-grounds wherein the mountain people rest after their narrow lives. It was unhedged, uncared for, and a few crumbling boards for headstones told the living generation where the dead were at rest. For a moment they paused to look at a spot under a great beech where the earth had been lately disturbed.

"It air shorely hard to see," said one in a low, slow voice, "why she was taken, 'n' him left; why she should hev to give her life fer the life he took. But He knows, He knows," the mountaineer continued, with unfaltering trust; and then, after a moment's struggle to reconcile fact with faith: "The Lord took whut He keered fer most, 'n' she was ready, 'n' he wasn't."

The other made no reply, and they kept on in silence. Upon a spur of the mountain beneath which the little mining-town had sunk to quiet for the night they parted with a hand-clasp. Not till then was the silence broken.

"Thar seems to be a penalty fer lovin' too

much down hyar," said one; "'n' I reckon," he added, slowly, "that both of us hev got hit to pay."

Turning, the speaker retraced his steps. The other kept on toward the lights below.

A CUMBERLAND VENDETTA

TO

MINERVA

AND

ELIZABETH

I

THE cave had been their hiding-place as children; it was a secret refuge now against hunger or darkness when they were hunting in the woods. The primitive meal was finished; ashes were raked over the red coals; the slice of bacon and the little bag of meal were hung high against the rock wall; and the two stepped from the cavern into a thicket of rhododendrons.

Parting the bushes toward the dim light, they stood on a massive shoulder of the mountain, the river girding it far below, and the afternoon shadows at their feet. Both carried guns—the tall mountaineer, a Winchester; the boy, a squirrel rifle longer than himself. Climbing about the rocky spur, they kept the same level over log and bowlder and through bushy ravine to the north. In half an hour, they ran into a path that led up home from the river, and they stopped to rest on a cliff that sank in a solid black wall straight under them. The sharp edge of a steep corn-field ran near, and, stripped of blade and tassel, the stalks and hooded ears looked in the coming dusk a little like monks at prayer. In the sunlight across the river the corn stood thin and frail. Over there a drought was on it; and when drifting thistle-plumes marked the noontide of the year, each yellow stalk had withered blades and an empty sheath. Everywhere a look of vague trouble lay upon the face of the mountains, and when the wind blew, the silver of the leaves showed ashen. Autumn was at hand.

There was no physical sign of kinship between the two, half-brothers though they were. The tall one was dark; the boy, a foundling, had flaxen hair, and was stunted and slender. He was a dreamy-looking little fellow, and one may easily find his like throughout the Cumberland —paler than his fellows, from staying much indoors, with half-haunted face, and eyes that are deeply pathetic when not cunning; ignorantly credited with idiocy and uncanny powers; treated with much forbearance, some awe, and a little contempt; and suffered to do his pleasure—nothing, or much that is strange—without comment.

"I tell ye, Rome," he said, taking up the thread of talk that was broken at the cave, "when Uncle Gabe says *he's* afeard thar's trouble comin', hit's a-comin'; 'n' I want you to git me a Winchester. I'm a-gittin' big enough now. I kin shoot might' nigh as good as you, 'n' whut am I fit fer with this hyeh old pawpaw pop-gun?"

"I don't want you fightin', boy, I've told ye. Y'u air too little 'n' puny, 'n' I want ye to stay home 'n' take keer o' mam 'n' the cattle— ef fightin' does come, I reckon thar won't be much."

"Don't ye?" cried the boy, with sharp contempt—"with ole Jas Lewallen a-devilin' Uncle Rufe, 'n' that blackheaded young Jas a-climbin' on stumps over thar 'cross the river, 'n' crowin' 'n' sayin' out open in Hazlan that ye air afeard o' him? Yes; 'n' he called me a idgit." The boy's voice broke into a whimper of rage.

"Shet up, Isom! Don't you go gittin' mad now. You'll be sick ag'in. I'll tend to him when the time comes." Rome spoke with rough kindness, but ugly lines had gathered at his mouth and forehead. The boy's tears came and went easily. He drew his sleeve across his eyes, and looked up the river. Beyond the bend, three huge birds rose into the sunlight and floated toward them. Close at hand, they swerved sidewise.

"They hain't buzzards," he said, standing up, his anger gone; "look at them straight wings!"

Again the eagles swerved, and two shot across the river. The third dropped with shut wings to the bare crest of a gaunt old poplar under them.

"Hit's a young un, Rome!" said the boy, excitedly. "He's goin' to wait thar tell the old uns come back. Gimme that gun!"

Catching up the Winchester, he slipped over the ledge; and Rome leaned suddenly forward, looking down at the river.

A group of horsemen had ridden around the bend, and were coming at a walk down the other shore. Every man carried something across his saddle-bow. There was a gray horse among them — young Jasper's — and an evil shadow came into Rome's face, and quickly passed. Near a strip of woods the gray turned up the mountain from the party, and on its back he saw the red glint of a woman's dress. With a half-smile he watched the scarlet figure ride from the woods, and climb slowly up through the sunny corn. On the spur above and full in the rich yellow light, she halted, half turning in her saddle. He rose to his feet, to his full height, his head bare, and thrown far back between his big shoulders, and, still as statues, the man and the woman looked at each other across the gulf of darkening air. A full minute the woman sat motionless, then rode on. At the edge of the woods she stopped and turned again.

A CUMBERLAND VENDETTA

The eagle under Rome leaped one stroke in
the air, and dropped like a clod into the sea of
leaves. The report of the gun and a faint cry
of triumph rose from below. It was good
marksmanship, but on the cliff Rome did not
heed it. Something had fluttered in the air
above the girl's head, and he laughed aloud.
She was waving her bonnet at him.

II

JUST where young Stetson stood, the mountains racing along each bank of the Cumberland had sent out against each other, by mutual impulse, two great spurs. At the river's brink they stopped sheer, with crests uplifted, as though some hand at the last moment had hurled them apart, and had led the water through the breach to keep them at peace. To-day the crags looked seamed by thwarted passion; and, sullen with firs, they made fit symbols of the human hate about the base of each.

When the feud began, no one knew. Even the original cause was forgotten. Both families had come as friends from Virginia long ago, and had lived as enemies nearly half a century. There was hostility before the war, but, until then, little bloodshed. Through the hatred of change, characteristic of the mountaineer the world over, the Lewallens were for the Union. The Stetsons owned a few slaves, and they fought for them. Peace found both still neighbors and worse foes. The war armed them,

and brought back an ancestral contempt for human life; it left them a heritage of lawlessness
that for mutual protection made necessary the
very means used by their feudal forefathers;
personal hatred supplanted its dead issues, and
with them the war went on. The Stetsons had a
good strain of Anglo-Saxon blood, and owned
valley-lands; the Lewallens kept store and made
" moonshine "; so kindred and debtors and kindred and tenants were arrayed with one or the
other leader, and gradually the retainers of both
settled on one or the other side of the river. In
time of hostility the Cumberland came to be
the boundary between life and death for the
dwellers on each shore. It was feudalism born
again.

Above one of the spurs each family had its
home; the Stetsons, under the seared face of
Thunderstruck Knob; the Lewallens, just beneath the wooded rim of Wolf's Head. The
eaves and chimney of each cabin were faintly
visible from the porch of the other. The first
light touched the house of the Stetsons; the
last, the Lewallen cabin. So there were times
when the one could not turn to the sunrise nor
the other to the sunset but with a curse in
his heart, for his eye must fall on the home of
his enemy.

For years there had been peace. The death

of Rome Stetson's father from ambush, and the
fight in the court-house square, had forced it.
After that fight only four were left—old Jasper
Lewallen and young Jasper, the boy Rome and
his uncle, Rufe Stetson. Then Rufe fled to the
West, and the Stetsons were helpless. For
three years no word was heard of him, but the
hatred burned in the heart of Rome's mother,
and was traced deep in her grim old face while
she patiently waited the day of retribution. It
smouldered, too, in the hearts of the women of
both clans who had lost husbands or sons or
lovers; and the friends and kin of each had little
to do with one another, and met and passed
with watchful eyes. Indeed, it would take so
little to turn peace to war that the wonder was
that peace had lived so long. Now trouble was
at hand. Rufe Stetson had come back at last, a
few months since, and had quietly opened store
at the county-seat, Hazlan—a little town five
miles up the river, where Troubled Fork runs
seething into the Cumberland—a point of neu-
trality for the factions, and consequently a bat-
tle-ground. Old Jasper's store was at the other
end of the town, and the old man had never been
known to brook competition. He had driven
three men from Hazlan during the last term
of peace for this offence, and everybody knew
that the fourth must leave or fight. Already

A CUMBERLAND VENDETTA

Rufe Stetson had been warned not to appear outside his door after dusk. Once or twice his wife had seen skulking shadows under the trees across the road, and a tremor of anticipation ran along both banks of the Cumberland.

III

A FORTNIGHT later, court came. Rome was going to Hazlan, and the feeble old Stetson mother limped across the porch from the kitchen, trailing a Winchester behind her. Usually he went unarmed, but he took the gun now, as she gave it, in silence.

The boy Isom was not well, and Rome had told him to ride the horse. But the lad had gone on afoot to his duties at old Gabe Bunch's mill, and Rome himself rode down Thunderstruck Knob through the mist and dew of the early morning. The sun was coming up over Virginia, and through a dip in Black Mountain the foot-hills beyond washed in blue waves against its white disk. A little way down the mountain, the rays shot through the gap upon him, and, lancing the mist into tatters, and lighting the dew-drops, set the birds singing. Rome rode, heedless of it all, under primeval oak and poplar, and along rain-clear brooks and happy waterfalls, shut in by laurel and rhododendron, and singing past mossy stones and lacelike ferns that brushed his stirrup. On the brow of every

128

cliff he would stop to look over the trees and the river to the other shore, where the gray line of a path ran aslant Wolf's Head, and was lost in woods above and below.

At the river he rode up-stream, looking still across it. Old Gabe Bunch hallooed to him from the doorway of the mill, as he splashed through the creek, and Isom's thin face peered through a breach in the logs. At the ford beyond, he checked his horse with a short oath of pleased surprise. Across the water, a scarlet dress was moving slowly past a brown field of corn. The figure was bonneted, but he knew the girl's walk and the poise of her head that far away. Just who she was, however, he did not know, and he sat irresolute. He had seen her first a month since, paddling along the other shore, erect, and with bonnet off and hair down; she had taken the Lewallen path up the mountain. Afterward, he saw her going at a gallop on young Jasper's gray horse, bareheaded again, and with her hair loose to the wind, and he knew she was one of his enemies. He thought her the girl people said young Jasper was going to marry, and he had watched her the more closely. From the canoe she seemed never to notice him; but he guessed, from the quickened sweep of her paddle, that she knew he was looking at her, and once, when he halted on his way home up the mountain, she half turned in her saddle and looked across at him. This happened again, and then she waved her bonnet at him. It was bad enough, any Stetson seeking any Lewallen for a wife, and for him to court young Jasper's sweetheart—it was a thought to laugh at. But the mischief was done. The gesture thrilled him, whether it meant defiance or good-will, and the mere deviltry of such a courtship made him long for it at every sight of her with the river between them. At once he began to plan how he should get near her, but, through some freak, she had paid no further heed to him. He saw her less often—for a week, indeed, he had not seen her at all till this day—and the forces that hindrance generates in an imperious nature had been at work within him. The chance now was one of gold, and with his life in his hand he turned into the stream. Across, he could see something white on her - shoulder—an empty bag. It was grinding-day, and she was going to the mill—the Lewallen mill. She stopped as he galloped up, and turned, pushing back her bonnet with one hand; and he drew rein. But the friendly, expectant light in her face kindled to such a blaze of anger in her eyes that he struck his horse violently, as though the beast had stopped of its own accord, and, cursing himself, kept on. A little farther, he halted again. Three horsemen, armed with Winchesters, were jogging along toward town ahead of him, and he wheeled about sharply. The girl, climbing rapidly toward Steve Brayton's cabin, was out of the way, but he was too late to reach the ford again. Down the road two more Lewallens with guns were in sight, and he lashed his horse into the stream where the water was deep. Old Gabe, looking from the door of his mill, quit laughing to himself; and under cover of the woods, the girl watched man and horse fighting the tide. Twice young Stetson turned his head. But his enemies apparently had not seen him, and horse and rider scrambled up the steep bank and under shelter of the trees. The girl had evidently learned who he was. Her sudden anger was significant, as was the sight of the Lewallens going armed to court, and Rome rode on, uneasy.

When he reached Troubled Fork, in sight of Hazlan, he threw a cartridge into place and shifted the slide to see that it was ready for use. Passing old Jasper's store on the edge of the town, he saw the old man's bushy head through the open door, and Lewallens and Braytons crowded out on the steps and looked after him. All were armed. Twenty paces farther he met young Jasper on his gray, and the look on his enemy's face made him grip his rifle. With a flashing cross-fire from eye to eye, the two passed, each with his thumb on the hammer of his Winchester. The groups on the court-house steps stopped talking as he rode by, and turned to look at him. He saw none of his own friends, and he went on at a gallop to Rufe Stetson's store. His uncle was not in sight. Steve Marcum and old Sam Day stood in the porch, and inside a woman was crying. Several Stetsons were near, and all with grave faces gathered about him.

He knew what the matter was before Steve spoke. His uncle had been driven from town. A last warning had come to him on the day before. The hand of a friend was in the caution, and Rufe rode away at dusk. That night his house was searched by men masked and armed. The Lewallens were in town, and were ready to fight. The crisis had come.

IV

BACK at the mill old Gabe was troubled. Usually he sat in a cane-bottomed chair near the hopper, whittling, while the lad tended the mill, and took pay in an oaken toll-dish smooth with the use of half a century. But the incident across the river that morning had made the old man uneasy, and he moved restlessly from his chair to the door, and back again, while the boy watched him, wondering what the matter was, but asking no questions. At noon an old mountaineer rode by, and the miller hailed him.

" Any news in town? " he asked.

" Hain't been to town. Reckon fightin' 's goin' on thar from whut I heerd." The careless, high-pitched answer brought the boy with wide eyes to the door.

" Whut d'ye hear? " asked Gabe.

" Jes heerd fightin' 's goin' on! "

Then every man who came for his meal brought a wild rumor from town, and the old miller moved his chair to the door, and sat there whittling fast, and looking anxiously toward

Hazlan. The boy was in a fever of unrest, and old Gabe could hardly keep him in the mill. In the middle of the afternoon the report of a rifle came down the river, breaking into echoes against the cliffs below, and Isom ran out the door, and stood listening for another, with an odd contradiction of fear and delight on his eager face. In a few moments Rome Stetson galloped into sight, and, with a shrill cry of relief, the boy ran down the road to meet him, and ran back, holding by a stirrup. Young Stetson's face was black with passion, and his eyes were heavy with drink. At the door of the mill he swung from his horse, and for a moment was hardly able to speak from rage. There had been no fight. The Stetsons were few and unprepared. They had neither the guns nor, without Rufe, the means to open the war, and they believed Rufe had gone for arms. So they had chafed in the store all day, and all day Lewallens on horseback and on foot were in sight; and each was a taunt to every Stetson, and, few as they were, the young and hot-headed wanted to go out and fight. In the afternoon a tale-bearer had brought some of Jasper's boasts to Rome, and, made reckless by moonshine and much brooding, he sprang up to lead them. Steve Marcum, too, caught up his gun, but old Sam's counsel checked him, and the two by force held

Rome back. A little later the Lewallens left town. The Stetsons, too, disbanded, and on the way home a last drop of gall ran Rome's cup of bitterness over. Opposite Steve Brayton's cabin a jet of smoke puffed from the bushes across the river, and a bullet furrowed the road in front of him. That was the shot they had heard at the mill. Somebody was drawing a "dead-line," and Rome wheeled his horse at the brink of it. A mocking yell came over the river, and a gray horse flashed past an open space in the bushes. Rome knew the horse and knew the yell; young Jasper was "bantering" him. Nothing maddens the mountaineer like this childish method of insult; and telling of it, Rome sat in a corner, and loosed a torrent of curses against young Lewallen and his clan.

Old Gabe had listened without a word, and the strain in his face was eased. Always the old man had stood for peace. He believed it had come after the court-house fight, and he had hoped against hope, even when Rufe came back to trade against old Jasper; for Rufe was big and good-natured, and unsuspected of resolute purpose, and the Lewallens' power had weakened. So, now that Rufe was gone again, the old miller half believed he was gone for good. Nobody was hurt; there was a chance yet for peace, and with a rebuke on his tongue and relief in his face, the old man sat back in his chair and went on whittling. The boy turned eagerly to a crevice in the logs and, trembling with excitement, searched the other bank for Jasper's gray horse, going home.

"He called me a idgit," he said to himself, with a threatening shake of his head. "Jes wouldn't *I* like to hev a chance at him! Rome ull git him! Rome ull git him!"

There was no moving point of white on the broad face of the mountains nor along the river road. Jasper was yet to come and, with ears alert to every word behind him, the lad fixed his eyes where he should see him first.

"Oh, he didn't mean to hit me. Not that he ain't mean enough to shoot from the bresh," Rome broke out savagely. "That's jes whut I'm afeard he will do. Thar was too much daylight fer him. Ef he jes don't come a-sneakin' over hyeh, 'n' waitin' in the lorrel atter dark fer me, it's all I axe."

"Waitin' in the lorrel!" Old Gabe could hold back no longer. "Hit's a shame, a burnin' shame! I don' know whut things air comin' to! 'Pears like all you young folks think about is killin' somebody. Folks usen to talk about how fer they could kill a deer; now it's how fer they kin kill a man. I hev knowed the time when a man would 'a' been druv out o' the

136

county fer drawin' a knife ur a pistol; 'n' ef a feller was' ever killed, it was kinder accidental, by a Barlow. I reckon folks got use' to weepons 'n' killin' 'n' bushwhackin' in the war. Looks like it's been gittin' wuss ever sence, 'n' now hit's dirk 'n' Winchester, 'n' shootin' from the bushes all the time. Hit's wuss 'n stealin' money to take a feller-creetur's life that way!"

The old miller's indignation sprang from memories of a better youth. For the courtesies of the code went on to the Blue Grass, and before the war the mountaineer fought with English fairness and his fists. It was a disgrace to use a deadly weapon in those days; it was a disgrace now not to use it.

"Oh, I know all the excuses folks make," he went on: "hit's fa'r fer one as 'tis fer t'other; y'u can't fight a man fa'r 'n' squar' who'll shoot you in the back; a pore man can't fight money in the couhts; 'n' thar hain't no witnesses in the lorrel but leaves; 'n' dead men don't hev much to say. I know it all. Hit's cur'us, but it act'-ally looks like lots o' decent young folks hev got usen to the idee—thar's so much of it goin' on, 'n' thar's so much talk 'bout killin' 'n' layin' out in the lorrel. Reckon folks 'll git to pesterin' women 'n' strangers bimeby, 'n' robbin' 'n' thievin'. Hit's bad enough thar's so leetle law thet folks hev to take it in their own hand•

oncet in a while, but this shootin' from the bresh—hit's p'int'ly a sin 'n' shame! Why," he concluded, pointing his remonstrance as he always did, " I seed your grandad and young Jas's fight up thar in Hazlan full two hours 'fore the war—fist and skull—'n' your grandad was whooped. *They* got up and shuk hands. I don't see why folks can't fight that way now. I wish Rufe 'n' old Jas 'n' you 'n' young Jas could have it out fist and skull, 'n' stop this killin' o' people like hogs. Thar's nobody left but you four. But thar's no chance o' that, I reckon."

" I'll fight him anyway, 'n' I reckon ef *he* don't die till *I* lay out in the lorrel fer *him*, he'll live a long time. Ef a Stetson ever done sech meanness as that I never heerd it."

" Nother hev I," said the old man, with quick justice. " You air a over-bearin' race, all o' ye, but I never knowed ye to be that mean. Hit's all the wus fer ye thet ye air in sech doin's. I tell ye, Rome——"

A faint cry rose above the drone of the millstones, and old Gabe stopped with open lips to listen. The boy's face was pressed close to the logs. A wet paddle had flashed into the sunlight from out the bushes across the river. He could just see a canoe in the shadows under them, and with quick suspicion his brain pictured Jas-

138

per's horse hitched in the bushes, and Jasper stealing across the river to waylay Rome. But the canoe moved slowly out of sight downstream and toward the deep water, the paddler unseen, and the boy looked around with a weak smile. Neither seemed to have heard him. Rome was brooding, with his sullen face in his hands; the old miller was busy with his own thoughts; and the boy turned again to his watch.

Jasper did not come. Isom's eyes began to ache from the steady gaze, and now and then he would drop them to the water swirling beneath. A slow wind swayed the overhanging branches at the mouth of the stream, and under them was an eddy. Escaping this, the froth and bubbles raced out to the gleams beating the air from the sunlit river. He saw one tiny fleet caught; a mass of yellow scum bore down and, sweeping through bubbles and eddy, was itself struck into fragments by something afloat. A tremulous shadow shot through a space of sunlight into the gloom cast by a thicket of rhododendrons, and the boy caught his breath sharply. A moment more, and the shape of a boat and a human figure quivered on the water running under him. The stern of a Lewallen canoe swung into the basin, and he sprang to his feet.

" Rome! " The cry cut sharply through the drowsy air. " Thar he is! Hit's Jas! "

The old miller rose to his feet. The boy threw himself behind the sacks of grain. Rome wheeled for his rifle, and stood rigid before the door. There was a light step without, the click of a gun-lock within; a shadow fell across the doorway, and a girl stood at the threshold with an empty bag in her hand.

V

WITH a little cry she shrank back a step. Her face paled and her lips trembled, and for a moment she could not speak. But her eyes swept the group, and were fixed in two points of fire on Rome.

"Why don't ye shoot!" she asked, scornfully. "I hev heerd that the Stetsons have got to makin' war on women-folks, but I never believed it afore." Then she turned to the miller.

"Kin I git some more meal hyeh?" she asked. "Or have ye stopped sellin' to folks on t'other side?" she added, in a tone that sought no favor.

"You kin have all ye want," said old Gabe, quietly.

"The mill on Dead Crick is broke ag'in," she continued, "'n' co'n is skeerce on our side. We'll have to begin buyin' purty soon, so I thought I'd save totin' the co'n down hyeh." She handed old Gabe the empty bag.

"Well," said he, "as it air gittin' late, 'n' ye have to climb the mountain ag'in, I'll let ye have that comin' out o' the hopper now. Take a cheer."

The girl sat down in the low chair, and, loosening the strings of her bonnet, pushed it back from her head. An old-fashioned horn comb dropped to the floor, and when she stooped to pick it up she let her hair fall in a heap about her shoulders. Thrusting one hand under it, she calmly tossed the whole mass of chestnut and gold over the back of the chair, where it fell rippling like water through a bar of sunlight. With head thrown back and throat bared, she shook it from side to side, and, slowly coiling it, pierced it with the coarse comb. Then passing her hands across her forehead and temples, as women do, she folded them in her lap, and sat motionless. The boy, crouched near, held upon her the mesmeric look of a serpent. Old Gabe was peering covertly from under the brim of his hat, with a chuckle at his lips. Rome had fallen back to a corner of the mill, sobered, speechless, his rifle in a nerveless hand. The passion that fired him at the boy's warning had as swiftly gone down at sight of the girl, and her cutting rebuke made him hot again with shame. He was angry, too—more than angry—because he felt so helpless, a sensation that was new and stifling. The scorn of her face, as he remembered it that morning, hurt him again while he looked at her. A spirit of contempt was still in her eyes, and quivering about her thin lips

142

" ' Why don't ye shoot ? ' "

and nostrils. She had put him beneath further notice, and yet every toss of her head, every movement of her hands, seemed meant for him, to irritate him. And once, while she combed her hair, his brain whirled with an impulse to catch the shining stuff in one hand and to pinion both her wrists with the other, just to show her that he was master, and still would harm her not at all. But he shut his teeth, and watched her. Among mountain women the girl was more than pretty; elsewhere only her hair, perhaps, would have caught the casual eye. She wore red homespun and coarse shoes; her hands were brown and hardened. Her arms and shoulders looked muscular, her waist was rather large—being as nature meant it—and her face in repose had a heavy look. But the poise of her head suggested native pride and dignity; her eyes were deep, and full of changing lights; the scarlet dress, loose as it was, showed rich curves in her figure, and her movements had a certain childlike grace. Her brow was low, and her mouth had character; the chin was firm, the upper lip short, and the teeth were even and white.

"I reckon thar's enough to fill the sack, Isom," said the old miller, breaking the strained silence of the group. The girl rose and handed him a few pieces of silver.

"I reckon I'd better pay fer it all," she said. "I s'pose I won't be over hyeh ag'in."

Old Gabe gave some of the coins back.

"Y'u know whut my price al'ays is," he said.

"I'm obleeged," answered the girl, flushing. "Co'n hev riz on our side. I thought mebbe you charged folks over thar more, anyways."

"I sells fer the same, ef co'n is high ur low," was the answer. "This side or t'other makes no diff'unce to me. I hev frien's on both sides, 'n' I take no part in sech doin's as air a shame to the mountains."

There was a quick light of protest in the girl's dark eyes; but the old miller was honored by both factions, and without a word she turned to the boy, who was tying the sack.

"The boat's loose!" he called out, with the string between his teeth; and she turned again and ran out. Rome stood still.

"Kerry the sack out, boy, 'n' holp the gal." Old Gabe's voice was stern, and the young mountaineer doggedly swung the bag to his shoulders. The girl had caught the rope, and drawn the rude dugout along the shore.

"Who axed ye to do that?" she asked, angrily.

Rome dropped the bag into the boat, and merely looked her in the face.

"Look hyeh, Rome Stetson"—the sound of

his name from her lips almost startled him—
" I'll hev ye understan' that I don't want to be
bounden to you, nor none o' yer kin."

Turning, she gave an impatient sweep with
her paddle. The prow of the canoe dipped and
was motionless. Rome had caught the stern,
and the girl wheeled in hot anger. Her impulse
to strike may have been for the moment and no
longer, or she may have read swiftly no unkind-
ness in the mountaineer's steady look; for the
uplifted oar was stayed in the air, as though at
least she would hear him.

" I've got nothin' ag'in' *you*," he said, slowly,
" Jas Lewallen hev been threatenin' me, 'n' I
thought it was him, 'n' I was ready fer *him*,
when you come into the mill. I wouldn't hurt
you nur no other woman. Y'u ought to know
it, 'n' ye do know it."

The words were masterful, but said in a way
that vaguely soothed the girl's pride, and the
oar was let slowly into the water.

" I reckon y'u air a friend o' his," he added,
still quietly. " I've seed ye goin' up thar, but
I've got nothin' ag'in' ye, whoever ye be."

She turned on him a sharp look of suspicion.
" I reckon I do be a friend o' hisn," she said,
deliberately; and then she saw that he was in
earnest. A queer little smile went like a ray
of light from her eyes to her lips, and she gave

145

a quick stroke with her paddle. The boat shot into the current, and was carried swiftly toward the Cumberland. The girl stood erect, swaying through light and shadow like a great scarlet flower blowing in the wind; and Rome watched her till she touched the other bank. Swinging the sack out, she stepped lightly after it, and, without looking behind her, disappeared in the bushes.

The boy Isom was riding away when Rome, turned, and old Gabe was watching from the door of the mill.

"Who is that gal?" he asked, slowly. It seemed somehow that he had known her a long while ago. A puzzled frown overlay his face, and the old miller laughed.

"You a-axin' who she be, 'n' she a-axin who you be, 'n' both o' ye a-knowin' one 'nother sence ye was knee-high. Why, boy, hit's old Jasper's gal—Marthy!"

VI

IN a flash of memory Rome saw the girl as
vividly as when he last saw her years ago.
They had met at the mill, he with his father,
she with hers. There was a quarrel, and the
two men were held apart. But the old sore as
usual was opened, and a week later Rome's
father was killed from the brush. He remembered his mother's rage and grief, her calls for
vengeance, the uprising, the fights, plots, and
ambushes. He remembered the look the girl
had given him that long ago, and her look that
day was little changed.

When fighting began, she had been sent for
safety to the sister of her dead mother in another county. When peace came, old Jasper
married again and the girl refused to come
home. Lately the step-mother, too, had passed
away, and then she came back to live. All this
the old miller told in answer to Rome's questions as the two walked away in the twilight.
This was why he had not recognized her, and
why her face yet seemed familiar even when
he crossed the river that morning.

147

"Uncle Gabe, how do you reckon the gal knowed who I was?"

"She axed me."

"She axed *you!* Whar?"

"Over thar in the mill." The miller was watching the young mountaineer closely. The manner of the girl was significant when she asked who Rome was, and the miller knew but one reason possible for his foolhardiness that morning.

"Do you mean to say she have been over hyeh afore?"

"Why, yes, come to think about it, three or four times while Isom was sick, and whut she come fer I can't make out. The mill over thar wasn't broke long, 'n' why she didn't go thar or bring more co'n at a time, to save her the trouble o' so many trips, I can't see to save me."

Young Stetson was listening eagerly. Again the miller cast his bait.

"Mebbe she's spyin'."

Rome faced him, alert with suspicion; but old Gabe was laughing silently.

"Don't you be a fool, Rome. The gal comes and goes in that boat, 'n' she couldn't see a soul without my knowin' it. She seed ye ridin' by one day, 'n' she looked mighty cur'us when I tole her who ye was."

148

Old Gabe stopped his teasing, Rome's face was so troubled, and himself grew serious.

"Rome," he said, earnestly, "I wish to the good Lord ye wasn't in sech doin's. Ef that had been young Jas 'stid o' Marthy, I reckon ye would 'a' killed him right thar."

"I wasn't going to let him kill me," was the sullen answer.

The two had stopped at a rickety gate swinging open on the road. The young mountaineer was pushing a stone about with the toe of his boot. He had never before listened to remonstrance with such patience, and old Gabe grew bold.

"You've been drinkin' ag'in, Rome," he said, sharply, "'n' I know it. Hit's been moonshine that's whooped you Stetsons, not the Lewallens, long as I kin rickollect, 'n' it ull be moonshine ag'in ef ye don't let it alone."

Rome made no denial, no defence. "Uncle Gabe," he said slowly, still busied with the stone, "hev that gal been over hyeh sence y'u tol' her who I was?"

The old man was waiting for the pledge that seemed on his lips, but he did not lose his temper.

"Not till to-day," he said, quietly.

Rome turned abruptly, and the two separated with no word of parting. For a moment the

miller watched the young fellow striding away
under his rifle.

"I have been atter peace a good while," he
said to himself, "but I reckon thar's a bigger
hand a-workin' now than mine." Then he lifted
his voice. "Ef Isom's too sick to come down
to the mill to-morrer, I wish you'd come 'n' holp
me."

Rome nodded back over his shoulder, and
went on, with head bent, along the river road.
Passing a clump of pines at the next curve, he
pulled a bottle from his pocket.

"Uncle Gabe's about right, I reckon," he
said, half aloud; and he raised it above his head
to hurl it away, but checked it in mid-air. For
a moment he looked at the colorless liquid, then,
with quick nervousness, pulled the cork of sassa-
fras leaves, gulped down the pale moonshine, and
dashed the bottle against the trunk of a beech.
The fiery stuff does its work in a hurry. He
was thirsty when he reached the mouth of a
brook that tumbled down the mountain along
the pathway that would lead him home, and he
stooped to drink where the water sparkled in a
rift of dim light from overhead. Then he sat
upright on a stone, with his wide hat-brim curved
in a crescent over his forehead, his hands caught
about his knees, and his eyes on the empty air.

He was scarcely over his surprise that the girl

was young Lewallen's sister, and the discovery had wrought a curious change. The piquant impulse of rivalry was gone, and something deeper was taking its place. He was confused and a good deal troubled, thinking it all over. He tried to make out what the girl meant by looking at him from the mountain-side, by waving her bonnet at him, and by coming to old Gabe's mill when she could have gone to her own. To be sure, she did not know then who he was, and she had stopped coming when she learned; but why had she crossed again that day? Perhaps she too was bantering him, and he was at once angry and drawn to her; for her mettlesome spirit touched his own love of daring, even when his humiliation was most bitter —when she told him he warred on women; when he held out to her the branch of peace and she swept it aside with a stroke of her oar. But Rome was little conscious of the weight of subtle facts like these. His unseeing eyes went back to her as she combed her hair. He saw the color in her cheeks, the quick light in her eyes, the naked, full throat once more, and the wavering forces of his unsteady brain centred in a stubborn resolution—to see it all again. He would make Isom stay at home, if need be, and he would take the boy's place at the mill. If she came there no more, he would cross the river again. Come peace or war, be she friend or enemy, he would see her. His thirst was fierce again, and, with this half-drunken determination in his heart, he stooped once more to drink from the cheerful little stream. As he rose, a loud curse smote the air. The river, pressed between two projecting cliffs, was narrow at that point, and the oath came across the water. An instant later a man led a lamed horse from behind a bowlder, and stooped to examine its leg. The dusk was thickening, but Rome knew the huge frame and gray beard of old Jasper Lewallen. The blood beat in a sudden tide at his temples, and, half by instinct, he knelt behind a rock, and, thrusting his rifle through a crevice, cocked it softly.

Again the curse of impatience came over the still water, and old Jasper rose and turned toward him. The glistening sight caught in the centre of his beard. That would take him in the throat; it might miss, and he let the sight fall till the bullet would cut the fringe of gray hair into the heart. Old Jasper, so people said, had killed his father in just this way; he had driven his uncle from the mountains; he was trying now to revive the feud. He was the father of young Jasper, who had threatened his life, and the father of the girl whose contempt had cut him to the quick twice that day. Again her taunt leaped through his heated brain, and his boast to the old miller followed it. His finger trembled at the trigger.

"No; by ——, no ! " he breathed between his teeth; and old Jasper passed on, unharmed.

VII

NEXT day the news of Rufe Stetson's flight went down the river on the wind, and before nightfall the spirit of murder was loosed on both shores of the Cumberland. The more cautious warned old Jasper. The Stetsons were gaining strength again, they said; so were their feudsmen, the Marcums, enemies of the Braytons, old Jasper's kinspeople. Keeping store, Rufe had made money in the West, and money and friends right and left through the mountains. With all his good-nature, he was a persistent hater, and he was shrewd. He had waited the chance to put himself on the side of the law, and now the law was with him. But old Jasper laughed contemptuously. Rufe Stetson was gone again, he said, as he had gone before, and this time for good. Rufe had tried to do what nobody had done, or could do, while he was alive. Anyway, he was reckless, and he cared little if war did come again. Still, the old man prepared for a fight, and Steve Marcum on the other shore made ready for Rufe's return.

It was like the breaking of peace in feudal

days. The close kin of each leader were already about him, and now the close friends of each took sides. Each leader trading in Hazlan had debtors scattered through the mountains, and these rallied to aid the man who had befriended them. There was no grudge but served a pretext for partisanship in the coming war. Political rivalry had wedged apart two strong families, the Marcums and Braytons; a boundary line in dispute was a chain of bitterness; a suit in a country court had sown seeds of hatred. Sometimes it was a horse-trade, a fence left down, or a gate left open, and the trespassing of cattle; in one instance, through spite, a neighbor had docked the tail of a neighbor's horse—had "muled his critter," as the owner phrased the outrage. There was no old sore that was not opened by the crafty leaders, no slumbering bitterness that they did not wake to life. "Help us to revenge, and we will help you," was the whispered promise. So, had one man a grudge against another, he could set his foot on one or the other shore, sure that his enemy would be fighting for the other.

Others there were, friends of neither leader, who, under stress of poverty or hatred of work, would fight with either for food and clothes; and others still, the ne'er-do-wells and outlaws, who fought by the day or month for hire. Even

these were secured by one or the other faction,
for Steve and old Jasper left no resource un-
tried, knowing well that the fight, if there was
one, would be fought to a quick and decisive
end. The day for the leisurely feud, for patient
planning, and the slow picking off of men from
one side or the other, was gone. The people
in the Blue Grass, who had no feuds in their
own country, were trying to stop them in the
mountain. Over in Breathitt, as everybody
knew, soldiers had come from the " settlemints,"
had arrested the leaders, and had taken them to
the Blue Grass for the feared and hated ordeal
of trial by a jury of " bigoted furriners." On
the heels of the soldiers came a young preacher
up from the Jellico hills, half " citizen," half
" furriner," with long black hair and a scar
across his forehead, who was stirring up the people, it was said, " as though Satan was atter
them." Over there the spirit of the feud was
broken, and a good effect was already percep-
tible around Hazlan. In past days every pair
of lips was sealed with fear, and the non-comba-
tants left crops and homes, and moved down the
river, when trouble began. Now only the timid
considered this way of escape. Steve and old
Jasper found a few men who refused to enter
the fight. Several, indeed, talked openly against
the renewal of the feud, and somebody, it was

said, had dared to hint that he would send to the Governor for aid if it should break out again. But these were rumors touching few people.

For once again, as time and time again before, one bank of the Cumberland was arrayed with mortal enmity against the other, and old Gabe sat, with shaken faith, in the door of his mill. For years he had worked and prayed for peace, and for a little while the Almighty seemed lending aid. Now the friendly grasp was loosening, and yet the miller did all he could. He begged Steve Marcum to urge Rufe to seek aid from the law when the latter came back; and Steve laughed, and asked what justice was possible for a Stetson, with a Lewallen for a judge and Braytons for a jury. The miller pleaded with old Jasper, and old Jasper pointed to the successes of his own life.

"I hev triumphed ag'in' my enemies time 'n' ag'in," he said. "The Lord air on my side, 'n' I gits a better Christian ever' year." The old man spoke with the sincerity of a barbarism that has survived the dark ages, and, holding the same faith, the miller had no answer. It was old Gabe indeed who had threatened to send to the Governor for soldiers, and this he would have done, perhaps, had there not been one hope left, and only one. A week had gone, and there was no word from Rufe Stetson. Up on

Thunderstruck Knob the old Stetson mother
was growing pitiably eager and restless. Every
day she slipped like a ghost through the leafless
woods and in and out the cabin, kindling hatred.
At every dawn or dusk she was on her porch
peering through the dim light for Rufe Stetson.
Steve Marcum was ill at ease. Rome Stetson
alone seemed unconcerned, and his name was
on every gossiping tongue.

He took little interest and no hand in getting
ready for the war. He forbade the firing of a
gun till Rufe came back, else Steve should fight
his fight alone. He grew sullen and morose.
His old mother's look was a thorn in his soul,
and he stayed little at home. He hung about
the mill, and when Isom became bedfast, the
big mountaineer, who had never handled anything but a horse, a plough, or a rifle, settled himself, to the bewilderment of the Stetsons, into
the boy's duties, and nobody dared question him.
Even old Gabe jested no longer. The matter
was too serious.

Meanwhile the winter threw off the last slum-
brous mood of autumn, as a sleeper starts from
a dream. A fortnight was gone, and still no
message came from the absent leader. One
shore was restive, uneasy; the other confident,
mocking. Between the two, Rome Stetson
waited his chance at the mill.

VIII

DAY was whitening on the Stetson shore. Across the river the air was still sharp with the chill of dawn, and the mists lay like flocks of sheep under shelter of rock and crag. A peculiar cry radiated from the Lewallen cabin with singular resonance on the crisp air—the mountain cry for straying cattle. A soft low came from a distant patch of laurel, and old Jasper's girl, Martha, folded her hands like a conch at her mouth, and the shrill cry again startled the air.

"Ye better come, ye pieded cow-brute." Picking up a cedar piggin, she stepped from the porch toward the meek voice that had answered her. Temper and exertion had brought the quick blood to her face. Her head was bare, her thick hair was loosely coiled, and her brown arms were naked almost to the shoulder. At the stable a young mountaineer was overhauling his riding-gear.

"Air you goin' to ride the hoss to-day, Jas?" she asked, querulously.

"That's jes whut I was aimin' to do. I'm a-goin' to town."

"Well, I 'lowed I was goin' to mill to-day. The co'n is 'mos' gone."

"Well, y'u 'lowed wrong," he answered, imperturbably.

"Y'u're mean, Jas Lewallen," she cried, hotly; "that's whut ye air, mean—dog-mean!"

The young mountaineer looked up, whistled softly, and laughed. But when he brought his horse to the door an hour later there was a bag of corn across the saddle.

"As ye air so powerful sot on goin' to mill, whether or no, I'll leave this hyeh sack at the bend o' the road, 'n' ye kin git it thar. I'll bring the meal back ef ye puts it in the same place. I hates to see women-folks a-ridin' this horse. Hit spiles him."

The horse was a dapple-gray of unusual beauty, and as the girl reached out her hand to stroke his throat, he turned to nibble at her arm.

"I reckon he'd jes as lieve have me ride him as you, Jas," she said. "Me 'n' him have got to be great friends. Ye orter n't to be so stingy."

"Well, he ain't no hoss to be left out'n the bresh now, 'n' I hain't goin' to 'low it."

Old Jasper had lounged out of the kitchen door, and stood with his huge bulk against a shrinking pillar of the porch. The two men were much alike. Both had the same black, threatening brows meeting over the bridge of the nose. A kind of grim humor lurked about the old man's mouth, which time might trace about young Jasper's. The girl's face had no humor; the same square brows, apart and clearly marked, gave it a strong, serious cast, and while she had the Lewallen fire, she favored her mother enough, so the neighbors said, " to have a mighty mild, takin' way about her ef she wanted."

" You're right, Jas," the old mountaineer said; " the hoss air a sin 'n' temptation. Hit do me good ever' time I look at him. Thar air no sech hoss, I tell ye, this side o' the settlements."

The boy started away, and the old man followed, and halted him out of the girl's hearing.

" Tell Eli Crump 'n' Jim Stover to watch the Breathitt road close now," he said, in a low voice. " See all them citizens I tol' ye, 'n' tell 'em to be ready when I says the word. Thar's no tellin' whut's goin' to happen."

Young Jasper nodded his head, and struck his horse into a gallop. The old man lighted his pipe, and turned back to the house. The girl, bonnet in hand, was starting for the valley.

" Thar ain't no use goin' to Gabe Bunch's fer yer grist," he said. " The mill on Dead Crick's

161

a-runnin' ag'in, 'n' I don't want ye over thar axin favors, specially jes now."

" I lef' somethin' fer ye to eat, dad," she replied, " ef ye gits hungry before I git back."

" You heerd me? " he called after her, knitting his brows.

" Yes, dad; I heerd ye," she answered, adding to herself, " But I don't heed ye." In truth, the girl heeded nobody. It was not her way to ask consent, even her own, nor to follow advice. At the bend of the road she found the bag, and for an instant she stood wavering. An impulse turned her to the river, and she loosed the boat, and headed it across the swift, shallow water from the ford and straight toward the mill. At every stroke of her paddle the water rose above the prow of the boat, and, blown into spray, flew back and drenched her; the wind loosed her hair, and, tugging at her skirts, draped her like a statue; and she fought them, wind and water, with mouth set and a smile in her eyes. One sharp struggle still, where the creek leaped into freedom; the mouth grew a little firmer, the eyes laughed more, the keel grated on pebbles, and the boat ran its nose into the withered sedge on the Stetson shore.

A tall gray figure was pouring grain into the hopper when she reached the door of the mill. She stopped abruptly, Rome Stetson turned, and

again the two were face to face. No greeting
passed. The girl lifted her head with a little
toss that deepened the set look about the mountaineer's mouth; her lax figure grew tense as
though strung suddenly against some coming
harm, and her eyes searched the shadows without once resting on him.

"Whar's Uncle Gabe?" She spoke shortly, and as to a stranger.

"Gone to town," said Rome, composedly.
He had schooled himself for this meeting.

"When's he comin' back?"

"Not 'fore night, I reckon."

"Whar's Isom?"

"Isom's sick."

"Well, who's tendin' this mill?"

For answer he tossed the empty bag into the
corner and, without looking at her, picked up
another bag.

"I reckon ye see me, don't ye?" he asked,
coolly. "Hev a cheer, and rest a spell. Hit's
a purty long climb whar you come from."

The girl was confused. She stayed in the
doorway, a little helpless and suspicious. What
was Rome Stetson doing here? His mastery of
the situation, his easy confidence, puzzled and
irritated her. Should she leave? The mountaineer was a Stetson, a worm to tread on if it
crawled across the path. It would be like back-

ing down before an enemy. He might laugh at her after she was gone, and, at that thought, she sat down in the chair with composed face, looking through the door at the tumbling water, which broke with a thousand tints under the sun, but able still to see Rome, sidewise, as he moved about the hopper, whistling softly.

Once she looked around, fancying she saw a smile on his sober face. Their eyes came near meeting, and she turned quite away.

" Ever seed a body out'n his head? "

The girl's eyes rounded with a start of surprise.

" Well, it's plumb cur'us. Isom's been that way lately. Isom's sick, ye know. Uncle Gabe's got the rheumatiz, 'n' Isom's mighty fond o' Uncle Gabe, 'n' the boy pestered me till I come down to he'p him. Hit p'int'ly air strange to hear him talkin'. He's jes a-ravin' 'bout hell 'n' heaven, 'n' the sin o' killin' folks. You'd ha' thought he hed been convicted, though none o' our fambly hev been much atter religion. He says as how the wrath uv a livin' God is a-goin' to sweep these mount'ins, ef some mighty tall repentin' hain't done. Of co'se he got all them notions from Gabe. But Isom al'ays was quar, 'n' seed things hisself. He ain't no fool! "

The girl was listening. Morbidly sensitive

164

to the supernatural, she had turned toward him, and her face was relaxed with fear and awe.

"He's havin' dreams 'n' sech-like now, 'n' I reckon thar's nothing he's seed or heerd that he don' talk about. He's been a-goin' on about you," he added, abruptly. The girl's hands gave a nervous twitch. "Oh, he don't say nothin' ag'in' ye. I reckon he tuk a fancy to ye. Mam was plumb distracted, not knowin' whar he had seed ye. She thought it was like his other talk, 'n' I never let on—a-knowin' how mam was." A flush rose like a flame from the girl's throat to her hair. "But hit's this war," Rome went on in an unsteady tone, "that he talks most about, 'n' I'm sorry myself that trouble's a-comin'." He dropped all pretence now. "I've been a-watchin' fer ye over thar on t' other shore a good deal lately. I didn't know ye at fust, Marthy "—he spoke her name for the first time—"'n' Gabe says y'u didn't know me. I remembered ye, though, 'n' I want to tell ye now what I tol' ye then: I've got nothin' ag'in *you*. I was hopin' ye mought come over ag'in—hit was sorter cur'us that y'u was the same gal—the same gal———"

His self-control left him; he was halting in speech, and blundering he did not know where. Fumbling an empty bag at the hopper, he had

165

not dared to look at the girl till he heard her move. She had risen, and was picking up her bag. The hard antagonism of her face calmed him instantly.

"Hain't ye goin' to have yer grist ground?"

"Not hyeh," she answered, quickly.

"Why, gal——" He got no further. Martha was gone, and he followed her to the bank, bewildered.

The girl's suspicion, lulled by his plausible explanation, had grown sharp again. The mountaineer knew that she had been coming there. He was at the mill for another reason than to take the boy's place; and with swift intuition she saw the truth.

He got angry as she rode away—angry with himself that he had let her go; and the same half-tender, half-brutal impulse seized him as when he saw her first. This time he yielded. His horse was at hand, and the river not far below was narrow. The bridle-path that led to the Lewallen cabin swerved at one place to a cliff overlooking the river, and by hard riding and a climb of a few hundred feet on foot he could overtake her half-way up the mountain steep.

The plan was no more than shaped before he was in the saddle and galloping down the river. The set of his face changed hardly a line while he swam the stream, and, drenched to the waist, scaled the cliff. When he reached the spot, he found the prints of a woman's shoe in the dust of the path, going down. There were none returning, and he had not long to wait. A scarlet bit of color soon flashed through the gray bushes below him. The girl was without her bag of corn. She was climbing slowly, and was looking at the ground as though in deep thought. Reckless as she was, she had come to realize at last just what she had done. She had been pleased at first, as would have been any woman, when she saw the big mountaineer watching her, for her life was lonely. She had waved her bonnet at him from mere mischief. She hardly knew it herself, but she had gone across the river to find out who he was. She had shrunk from him as from a snake thereafter, and had gone no more until old Jasper had sent her because the Lewallen mill was broken, and because she was a woman, and would be safe from harm. She had met him then when she could not help herself. But now she had gone of her own accord. She had given this Stetson, a bitter enemy, a chance to see her, to talk with her. She had listened to him; she had been on the point of letting him grind her corn. And he knew how often she had gone to the mill, and he could not know that she had ever been sent. Perhaps he thought that she had come to make overtures of peace, friendship, even more. The suspicion reddened her face with shame, and her anger at him was turned upon herself. Why she had gone again that day she hardly knew. But if there was another reason than simple perversity, it was the memory of Rome Stetson's face when he caught her boat and spoke to her in a way she could not answer. The anger of the moment came with every thought of the incident afterward, and with it came too this memory of his look, which made her at once defiant and uneasy. She saw him now only when she was quite close, and, startled, she stood still; his stern look brought her the same disquiet, but she gave no sign of fear.

"Whut's the matter with ye?"

The question was too abrupt, too savage, and the girl looked straight at him, and her lips tightened with a resolution not to speak. The movement put him beyond control.

"Y'u puts hell into me, Marthy Lewallen; y'u puts downright hell into me." The words came between gritted teeth. "I want to take ye up 'n' throw ye off this cliff clean into the river, 'n' I reckon the next minute I'd jump off atter ye. Y'u've 'witched me, gal! I forgits who ye air 'n' who I be, 'n' sometimes I want

to come over hyeh 'n' kerry ye out'n these moun-
t'ins, 'n' nuver come back. You know whut
I've been watchin' the river fer sence the fust
time I seed ye. You know whut I've been
a-stayin' at the mill fer, 'n' Steve mad 'n' mam
a-jowerin'—'n' a-lookin' over hyeh fer ye night
'n' day! Y'u know whut I've jes swum over
hyeh fer! Whut's the matter with ye?"

Martha was not looking for a confession like
this. It took away her shame at once, and the
passion of it thrilled her, and left her trembling.
While he spoke her lashes drooped quickly, her
face softened, and the color came back to it.
She began intertwining her fingers, and would
not look up at him.

"Ef y'u hates me like the rest uv ye, why
don't ye say it right out? 'N' ef ye *do* hate me,
whut hev *you* been lookin' 'cross the river fer,
'n' a-shakin' yer bonnet at me, 'n' paddlin' to
Gabe's fer yer grist, when the mill on Dead
Crick's been a-runnin', 'n' I know it? You've
been banterin' me, hev ye?"—the blood rose
to his eyes again. "Ye mustn't fool with me,
gal, by ——, ye mustn't. Whut *hev* you been
goin' over thar fer?" He even took a threatening step toward her, and, with a helpless gesture, stopped. The girl was a little frightened.
Indeed, she smiled, seeing her power over him;
she seemed even about to laugh outright; but

169

the smile turned to a quick look of alarm, and she bent her head suddenly to listen to something below. At last she did speak. "Somebody's comin'!" she said. "You'd better git out o' the way," she went on, hurriedly. "Somebody's comin', I tell ye! Don't ye hear?"

It was no ruse to get rid of him. The girl's eyes were dilating. Something was coming far below. Rome could catch the faint beats of a horse's hoofs. He was unarmed, and he knew it was death for him to be seen on that forbidden mountain; but he was beyond caution, and ready to welcome any vent to his passion, and he merely shook his head.

"Ef it's Satan hisself, I hain't goin' to run." The hoof-beats came nearer. The rider must soon see them from the coil below.

"Rome, hit's Jas! He's got his rifle, and he'll kill ye, 'n' me too!" The girl was white with distress. She had called him by his name, and the tone was of appeal, not anger. The black look passed from his face, and he caught her by the shoulders with rough tenderness; but she pushed him away, and without a word he sprang from the road and let himself noiselessly down the cliff. The hoof-beats thundered above his head, and Young Jasper's voice hailed Martha.

170

"This hyeh's the bigges' meal I ever strad-
dled. Why d'n't ye git the grist ground?"

For a moment the girl did not answer, and
Rome waited, breathless. "Wasn't the mill
runnin'? Whyn't ye go on 'cross the river?"

"That's whut I did," said the girl, quietly.
"Uncle Gabe wasn't thar, 'n' Rome Stetson
was. I wouldn't 'low him to grin' the co'n, 'n'
so I toted hit back."

"Rome Stetson!" The voice was lost in a
volley of oaths.

The two passed out of hearing, and Rome
went plunging down the mountain, swinging
recklessly from one little tree to another, and
wrenching limbs from their sockets out of pure
physical ecstasy. When he reached his horse he
sat down, breathing heavily, on a bed of moss,
with a strange new yearning in his heart. If
peace should come! Why not peace, if Rufe
should not come back? He would be the leader
then, and without him there could be no war.
Old Jasper had killed his father. He was too
young at the time to feel poignant sorrow now,
and somehow he could look even at that death
in a fairer way. His father had killed old Jasper's brother. So it went back: a Lewallen
killed a Stetson; that Stetson had killed a Lewallen, until one end of the chain of deaths was
lost, and the first fault could not be placed,

though each clan put it on the other. In every generation there had been compromises—periods of peace; why not now? Old Gabe would gladly help him. He might make friends with young Jasper; he might even end the feud. And then—he and Martha—why not? He closed his eyes, and for one radiant moment it all seemed possible. And then a gaunt image rose in the dream, and only the image was left. It was the figure of his mother, stern and silent through the years, opening her grim lips rarely without some curse against the Lewallen race. He remembered she had smiled for the first time when she heard of the new trouble—the flight of his uncle and the hope of conflict. She had turned to him with her eyes on fire and her old hands clinched. She had said nothing, but he understood her look. And now—Good God! what would she think and say if she could know what he had done? His whole frame twitched at the thought, and, with a nervous spring to escape it, he was on his feet, and starting down the mountain.

Close to the river he heard voices below him, and he turned his horse quickly aside into the bushes. Two women who had been washing clothes passed, carrying white bundles home. They were talking of the coming feud.

"That ar young Stetson ain't much like his

dad," said one. " Young Jas has been a-darin'
'n' a-banterin' him, 'n' he *won't* take it up.
They say he air turnin' out a plumb coward."

When he reached the Stetson cabin three
horses with drooping heads were hitched to the
fence. All had travelled a long way. One
wore a man's saddle; on the others were thick
blankets tied together with leathern thongs.

In the dark porch sat several men. Through
the kitchen door he could see his mother getting
supper. Inside a dozen rifles leaned against the
wall in the firelight, and about their butts was a
pile of ammunition. In the doorway stood
Rufe Stetson.

IX

ALL were smoking and silent. Several spoke from the shadows as Rome stepped on the porch, and Rufe Stetson faced him a moment in the doorway, and laughed.

"Seem kinder s'prised?" he said, with a searching look. "Wasn't lookin' for me? I reckon I'll s'prise sev'ral ef I hev good-luck."

The subtlety of this sent a chuckle of appreciation through the porch, but Rome passed in without answer.

Isom lay on his bed within the circle of light, and his face in the brilliant glow was white, and his eyes shone feverishly. "Rome," he said, excitedly, "Uncle Rufe's hyeh, 'n' they laywayed him, 'n'——" He paused abruptly. His mother came in, and at her call the mountaineers trooped through the covered porch, and sat down to supper in the kitchen. They ate hastily and in silence, the mother attending their wants, and Rome helping her. The meal finished, they drew their chairs about the fire. Pipes were lighted, and Rufe Stetson rose and closed the door.

174

" Thar's no use harryin' the boy," he said;
" I reckon he'll be too puny to take a hand."

The mother stopped clearing the table, and
sat on the rock hearth close to the fire, her
withered lips shut tight about a lighted pipe,
and her sunken eyes glowing like the coal of
fire in its black bowl. Now and then she
would stretch her knotted hands nervously into
the flames, or knit them about her knees, looking closely at the heavy faces about her, which
had lightened a little with expectancy. Rufe
Stetson stood before the blaze, his hands clasped
behind him, and his huge figure bent in reflec-
tion. At intervals he would look with half-shut
eyes at Rome, who sat with troubled face outside the firelight. Across the knees of Steve
Marcum, the best marksman in the mountains,
lay the barrel of a new Winchester. Old Sam
Day, Rufe's father-in-law and counsellor to the
Stetsons for a score of years, sat as if asleep on
the opposite side of the fireplace from the old
mother, with his big square head pressed down
between his misshapen shoulders.

" The time hev come, Rome." Rufe spoke
between the puffs of his pipe, and Rome's heart
quickened, for every eye was upon him. Thar's
goin' to be trouble now. I hear as how young
Jasper hev been talkin' purty tall about ye—
'lowin' as how ye air afeard o' him."

Rome felt his mother's burning look. He did not turn toward her nor Rufe, but his face grew sullen, and his voice was low and harsh. " I reckon he'll find out about that when the time comes," he said, quietly—too quietly, for the old mother stirred uneasily, and significant glances went from eye to eye. Rufe did not look up from the floor. He had been told about Rome's peculiar conduct, and, while the reason for it was beyond guessing, he knew the temper of the boy and how to kindle it. He had thrust a thorn in a tender spot, and he let it rankle. How sorely it did rankle he little knew. The voice of the woman across the river was still in Rome's ears. Nothing cuts the mountaineer to the quick like the name of coward. It stung him like the lash of an ox-whip then; it smarted all the way across the river and up the mountain. Young Jasper had been charging him broadcast with cowardice, and Jasper's people no doubt believed it. Perhaps his own did —his uncle, his mother. The bare chance of such a humiliation set up an inward rage. He wondered how he could ever have been such a fool as to think of peace. The woman's gossip had swept kindly impulses from his heart with a fresh tide of bitterness, and, helpless now against its current, he sullenly gave way, and let his passions loose to drift with it.

"Whar d' ye git the guns, Rufe?" Steve was testing the action of the Winchester with a kindling look, as the click of the locks struck softly through the silence.

"Jackson; 'way up in Breathitt, at the eend of the new road."

"No wonder y'u've been gone so long."

"I had to wait thar fer the guns, 'n' I had to travel atter dark comin' back, 'n' lay out'n the bresh by day. Hit's full eighty mile up thar."

"Air ye shore nobody seed ye?"

The question was from a Marcum, who had come in late, and several laughed. Rufe threw back his dusty coat, which was ripped through the lapel by a bullet.

"They seed me well 'nough fer that," he said, grimly, and then he looked toward Rome, who thought of old Jasper, and gave back a gleam of fierce sympathy. There were several nods of approval along with the laugh that followed. It was a surprise—so little consideration of an escape so narrow—from Rufe; for, as old Gabe said, Rufe was big and good-natured, and was not thought fit for leadership. But there was a change in him when he came back from the West. He was quieter; he laughed less. No one spoke of the difference; it was too vague; but every one felt it, and it had an effect. His flight had made many un-

177

easy, but his return, for that reason, brought a stancher fealty from these; and this was evident now. All eyes were upon him, and all tongues, even old Sam's, waited now for his to speak.

"Whut we've got to do, we've got to do mighty quick," he began, at last. "Things air changin'. I seed it over thar in Breathitt. The soldiers 'n' that scar-faced Jellico preacher hev broke up the fightin' over thar, 'n' ef we don't watch out, they'll be a-doin' it hyeh, when we start our leetle frolic. We hain't got no time to fool. Old Jas knows this as well as me, 'n' thar's goin' to be mighty leetle chance fer 'em to layway 'n' pick us off from the bresh. Thar's goin' to be fa'r fightin' fer once, thank the Lord. They bushwhacked us durin' the war, 'n' they've laywayed us 'n' shot us to pieces ever sence; but now, ef God A'mighty's willin', the thing's a-goin' to be settled one way or t'other at last, I reckon."

He stopped a moment to think. The men's breathing could be heard, so quiet was the room, and Rufe went on telling in detail, slowly, as if to himself, the wrongs the Lewallens had done his people. When he came to old Jasper his voice was low, and his manner was quieter than ever.

"*Now* old Jas have got to the p'int whar he says as how nobody in this county kin undersell him 'n' stay hyeh. Old Jas druv Bond Vickers out'n the mount'ins fer tryin' hit. He druv Jess Hale away; 'n' them two air our kin."

The big mountaineer turned then, and knocked the ashes from his pipe. His eyes grew a little brighter, and his nostrils spread, but with a sweep of his arm he added, still quietly:

" Y' all know whut he's done."

The gesture lighted memories of personal wrongs in every breast; he had tossed a fire-brand among fagots, and an angry light began to burn from the eyes that watched him.

" Ye know, too, that he thinks he has played the same game with me; but ye don't know, I reckon, that he had ole Jim Stover 'n' that mis'-able Eli Crump a-hidin' in the bushes to shoot me "—again he grasped the torn lapel; " that a body warned me to git away from Hazlan; 'n' the night I left home they come thar to kill me, 'n' s'arched the house, 'n' skeered Mollie 'n' the leetle gal 'most to death."

The mountaineer's self-control was lost suddenly in a furious oath. The men did know, but in fresh anger they leaned forward in their chairs, and twisted about with smothered curses. The old woman had stopped smoking, and was rocking her body to and fro. Her lips were drawn in upon her toothless gums, and her pipe was clinched against her sunken breast. The head of the old mountaineer was lifted, and his eyes were open and shining fiercely.

"I hear as how he says I'm gone fer good. Well, I have been kinder easy-goin', hatin' to fight, but sence the day I seed Rome's dad thar dead in his blood, I hev had jes one thing I wanted to do. Thar wasn't no use stayin' hyeh; I seed that. Rome thar was too leetle, and they was too many fer me. I knowed it was easier to git a new start out West, 'n' when I come back to the mount'in, hit was to do *jes—whut I'm — going — to — do — now.*" He wheeled suddenly upon Rome, with one huge hand lifted. Under it the old woman's voice rose in a sudden wail:

"Yes; 'n' I want to see it done befoh I die. I hain't hyeh fer long, but I hain't goin' to leave as long as ole Jas is hyeh, 'n' I want ye all to know it. Ole Jas hev got to go fust. You hear me, Rome? I'm a-talkin' to you; I'm a-talkin' to you. Hit's yo' time now!"

The frenzied chant raised Rome from his chair. Rufe himself took up the spirit of it, and his voice was above all caution.

"Yes, Rome! They killed him, boy. They sneaked on him, 'n' shot him to pieces from the bushes. Yes; hit's yo' time now! Look hyeh, boys!" He reached above the fireplace and took down an old rifle—his brother's—which the old mother had suffered no one to touch. He held it before the fire, pointing to two crosses made near the flash-pan. "Thar's one fer ole Jim Lewallen! Thar's one fer ole Jas! He got Jim, but ole Jas has got him, 'n' thar's his cross thar yit! Whar's *yo'* gun, Rome? Shame on ye, boy!"

The wild-eyed old woman was before him. She had divined Rufe's purpose, and was already at his side, with Rome's Winchester in one hand and a clasp-knife in the other. Every man was on his feet; the door was open, and the boy Isom was at the threshold, his eyes blazing from his white face. Rome had strode forward.

"Yes, boy; now's the time, right hyeh before us all!"

The mother had the knife outstretched. Rome took it, and the scratch of the point on the hard steel went twice through the stillness— "one more fer the young un"; the voice was the old mother's—then twice again.

The moon was sinking when Rome stood in the door alone. The tramp of horses was growing fainter down the mountain. The trees were swaying in the wind below him, and he could just see the gray cliffs on the other shore. The morning seemed far away; it made him dizzy looking back to it through the tumult of the day. Somewhere in the haze was the vision of a girl's white face—white with distress for him. Her father and her brother he had sworn to kill. He had made a cross for each, and each cross was an oath. He closed the door; and then he gave way, and sat down with his head in both hands. The noises in the kitchen ceased. The fire died away, and the chill air gathered about him. When he rose, the restless eyes of the boy were upon him from the shadows.

X

IT was court-day in Hazlan, but so early in the morning nothing was astir in the town that hinted of its life on such a day. But for the ring of a blacksmith's anvil on the quiet air, and the fact that nowhere was a church-spire visible, a stranger would have thought that the peace of Sabbath overlay a village of God-fearing people. A burly figure lounged in the porch of a rickety house, and yawned under a swinging sign, the rude letters of which promised " private entertainment " for the traveller unlucky enough to pass that way. In the one long, narrow main street, closely flanked by log and framed houses, nothing else human was in sight. Out from this street, and in an empty square, stood the one brick building in the place, the court-house, brick without, brick within; unfinished, unpencilled, unpainted; panes out of the windows, a shutter off here and there, or swinging drunkenly on one hinge; the door wide open, as though there was no privacy within—a poor structure, with the look of a good man gone shiftless and fast going wrong.

A CUMBERLAND VENDETTA

Soon two or three lank brown figures appeared from each direction on foot; then a horseman or two, and by and by mountaineers came in groups, on horse and on foot. In time the side alleys and the court-house square were filled with horses and mules, and even steers. The mountaineers crowded the narrow street: idling from side to side; squatting for a bargain on the wooden sidewalks; grouping on the porch of the rickety hotel, and on the court-house steps; loitering in and out of the one store in sight. Out in the street several stood about a horse, looking at his teeth, holding his eyes to the sun, punching his ribs, twisting his tail; while the phlegmatic owner sat astride the submissive beast, and spoke short answers to rare questions. Everybody talked politics, the crop failure, or the last fight at the seat of some private war; but nobody spoke of a Lewallen or a Stetson unless he knew his listener's heart, and said it in a whisper. For nobody knew when the powder would flash, or who had taken sides, or that a careless word might not array him with one or the other faction.

A motley throng it was—in brown or gray homespun, with trousers in cowhide boots, and slouched hats with brims curved according to temperament, but with striking figures in it; the patriarch with long, white hair, shorn even with the base of the neck, and bearded only at the throat—a justice of the peace, and the sage of his district; a little mountaineer with curling black hair and beard, and dark, fine features; a grizzled giant with a head rugged enough to have been carelessly chipped from stone; a bragging candidate claiming everybody's notice; a square-shouldered fellow surging through the crowd like a stranger; an open-faced, devil-may-care young gallant on fire with moonshine; a skulking figure with brutish mouth and shifting eyes. Indeed, every figure seemed distinct; for, living apart from his neighbor, and troubling the law but little in small matters of dispute, the mountaineer preserves independence, and keeps the edges of his individuality unworn. Apparently there was not a woman in town. Those that lived there kept housed, and the fact was significant. Still, it was close to noon, and yet not a Stetson or a Lewallen had been seen. The stores of Rufe and old Jasper were at the extremities of the town, and the crowd did not move those ways. It waited in the centre, and whetted impatience by sly trips in twos and three to stables or side alleys for " mountain dew." Now and then the sheriff, a little man with a mighty voice, would appear on the court-house steps, and summon a witness to court, where a frightened judge gave instructions to a frightened jury. But few went, unless called; for the interest was outside; every man in the streets knew that a storm was nigh, and was waiting to see it burst.

Noon passed. A hoarse bell and a whining hound had announced dinner in the hotel. The guests were coming again into the streets. Eyes were brighter, faces a little more flushed, and the " moonshine " was passed more openly. Both ways the crowd watched closely. The quiet at each end of the street was ominous, and the delay could last but little longer. The lookers-on themselves were getting quarrelsome. The vent must come soon, or among them there would be trouble.

"Thar comes Jas Lewallen!" At last. A dozen voices spoke at once. A horseman had appeared far down the street from the Lewallen end. The clouds broke from about the sun, and a dozen men knew the horse that bore him; for the gray was prancing the street sidewise, and throwing the sunlight from his flanks. Nobody followed, and the crowd was puzzled. Young Jasper carried a Winchester across his saddle-bow, and, swaying with the action of his horse, came on.

" What air he about? "

" He's a plumb idgit."

" He mus' be crazy."

A CUMBERLAND VENDETTA

" He's drunk! "

The wonder ceased. Young Jasper was
reeling. Two or three Stetsons slipped from ·
the crowd, and there was a galloping of hoofs
the other way. Another horseman appeared
from the Lewallen end, riding hastily. The
new-comer's errand was to call Jasper back.
But the young dare-devil was close to the
crowd, and was swinging a bottle over his head.

" Come back hyeh, Jas! Come hyeh! "
The new-comer was shouting afar off while he
galloped. Horses were being untethered from
the side alleys. Several more Lewallen riders
came in sight. They could see the gray shining
in the sunlight amid the crowd, and the man
sent after him halted at a safe distance, gesticu-
lating; and they, too, spurred forward.

" Hello, boys! " young Jasper was calling
out, as he swayed from side to side, the people
everywhere giving him way.

" Fun to-day, by ——! fun to-day! Who'll
hev a drink? Hyeh's hell to the Stetsons, whar
some of 'em 'll be afore night! "

With a swagger he lifted the bottle to his
lips, and, stopping short, let it fall untouched to
the ground. He had straightened in his saddle,
and was looking up the street. With a deep
curse he threw the Winchester to his shoulder,
fired, and before his yell had died on his lips

187

horse and rider were away like a shaft of light. The crowd melted like magic from the street. The Stetsons, chiefly on foot, did not return the fire, but halted up the street, as if parleying. Young Jasper joined his party, and they, too, stood still a moment, puzzled by the irresolution of the other side.

"Watch out! they're gittin' round ye! Run for the court-house, ye fools!—ye, run!" The voice came in a loud yell from somewhere down the street, and its warning was just in time.

A wreath of smoke came about a corner of the house far down the street, and young Jasper yelled, and dashed up a side alley with his followers. A moment later judge, jury, witnesses, and sheriff were flying down the court-house steps at the point of Lewallen guns; the Lewallen horses, led by the gray, were snorting through the streets; their riders, barricaded in the forsaken court-house, were puffing a stream of fire and smoke from every window of court-room below and jury-room above.

The streets were a bedlam. The Stetsons were yelling with triumph. The Lewallens were divided, and Rufe placed three Stetsons with Winchesters on each side of the court-house, and kept them firing. Rome, pale and stern, hid his force between the square and the Lewallen store. He was none too quick. The rest were coming on, led by old Jasper. It was reckless, riding that way right into death; but the old man believed young Jasper's life at stake, and the men behind asked no questions when old Jasper led them. The horses' hoofs beat the dirt street like the crescendo of thunder. The fierce old man's hat was gone, and his mane-like hair was shaking in the wind. Louder—and still the Stetsons were quiet—quiet too long. The wily old man saw the trap, and, with a yell, whirled the column up an alley, each man flattening over his saddle. From every window, from behind every corner and tree, smoke belched from the mouth of a Winchester. Two horses went down; one screamed; the other struggled to his feet, and limped away with an empty saddle. One of the fallen men sprang into safety behind a house, and one lay still, with his arms stretched out and his face in the dust.

From behind barn, house, and fence the Lewallens gave back a scattering fire; but the Stetsons crept closer, and were plainly in greater numbers. Old Jasper was being surrounded, and he mounted again, and all, followed by a chorus of bullets and triumphant yells, fled for a wooded slope in the rear of the court-house. A dozen Lewallens were prisoners, and must give up or starve. There was savage joy in the Stetson crowd, and many-footed rumor went all ways that night.

Despite sickness and Rome's strict order, Isom had ridden down to the mill. Standing in the doorway, he and old Gabe saw up the river, where the water broke into foam over the ford, a riderless gray horse plunging across. Later it neighed at a gate under Wolf's Head, and Martha Lewallen ran out to meet it. Across under Thunderstruck Knob that night the old Stetson mother listened to Isom's story of the fight with ghastly joy in her death-marked face.

XI

ALL night the court-house was guarded and on guard. At one corner of the square Rufe Stetson, with a few men, sat on watch in old Sam Day's cabin—the fortress of the town, built for such a purpose, and used for it many times before. The prisoners, too, were alert, and no Stetson ventured into the open square, for the moon was high; an exposure any-where was noted instantly by the whistle of a rifle-ball, and the mountaineer takes few risks except under stress of drink or passion. Rome Stetson had placed pickets about the town wherever surprise was possible. All night he patrolled the streets to keep his men in such readiness as he could for the attack that the Lewallens would surely make to rescue their living friends and to avenge the dead ones.

But the triumph was too great and unexpect-ed. Two Braytons were dead; several more were prisoners with young Jasper in the court-house; and drinking began.

As the night deepened without attack the Stetsons drank more, and grew reckless. A dance was started. Music and "moonshine" were given to every man who bore a Winchester. The night was broken with drunken yells, the random discharge of fire-arms, and the monotone of heavy feet. The two leaders were helpless, and the inaction of the Lewallens puzzled them. Chafed with anxiety, they kept their eyes on the court-house or on the thicket of gloom where their enemies lay. But the woods were as quiet as the pall of shadows over them. Once Rome, making his rounds, saw a figure crawling through a field of corn. It looked like Crump's, but before he could fire the man rolled like a ball down the bushy bank to the river. An instant later some object went swiftly past a side street—somebody on horseback—and a picket fired an alarm. The horse kept on, and Rome threw his rifle on a patch of moonlight, but when the object flashed through, his finger was numbed at the trigger. In the moonlight the horse looked gray, and the rider was seated sidewise. A bullet from the court-house clipped his hat-brim as he ran recklessly across the street to where Steve Marcum stood in the dark behind old Sam's cabin.

"Jim Hale 'll git him as he goes up the road," said Steve, calmly—and then with hot impatience, "Why the hell don't he shoot?"

Rome started forward in the moonlight, and

Steve caught his arm. Two bullets hissed from the court-house, and he fell back.

A shot sounded from the bushes far away from the road. The horse kept on, and splashed into Troubled Fork, and Steve swore bitterly.

"Hit hain't Jim. Hit's that mis'able Bud Vickers; he's been a-standin' guard out'n the bushes 'stid o' the road. That was a spy, I tell ye, 'n' the coward let him in and let him out. They'll know now we're all drunk! Whut's the matter?"

Rome's mouth was half open. He looked white and sick, and Steve thought he had been hit, but he took off his hat. "Purty close!" he said, with a laugh, pointing at the bullet-hole through the brim.

Steve, unsuspicious, went on: "Hit was a spy, I tell ye. Bud was afeard to stan' in the road, 'n' I'm goin' out thar 'n' twist his damned neck. We've got 'em, Rome! I tell ye, we've got 'em! Ef we kin git through this night, and git the boys sober in the morning, we've got 'em shore!"

The night did pass in safety, darkness wore away without attack, and morning broke on the town in its drunken stupor. Then the curious silence of the Lewallens was explained. The rumor came that old Jasper was dead, and it went broadcast. Later, friends coming to the edge of the town for the bodies of the dead Lewallens confirmed it. A random ball had passed through old Lewallen's body in the wild flight for the woods, and during the night he had spent his last breath in a curse against the man who fired it.

Then each Stetson, waked from his drunken sleep, drank again when he heard of the death. The day bade fair to be like the night, and again the anxiety of the leaders was edged with fear. Old Jasper dead and young Jasper a prisoner, the chance was near to end the feud, or there would be no Lewallen left to lead their enemies. But, again, they were wellnigh helpless. Already they had barely enough men to guard their prisoners. Of the Marcums, Steve alone was able to handle a Winchester, and outside the sounds of the carousal were in the air and growing louder. In a little while, if the Lewallens but knew it, escape would be easy and the Stetsons could be driven from the town.

"Oh, they know it," said Steve. "They'll be a-whoopin' down out o' them woods purty soon, 'n' we're goin' to ketch hell. I'd like to know mighty well who that spy was last night. That cussed Bud Vickers says it was a ha'nt, on a white hoss, with long hair flyin' in the wind, 'n' that he shot plumb through it. I jus' wish I'd a had a chance at it."

Still, noon came again without trouble, and the imprisoned Lewallens had been twenty-four hours without food. Their ammunition was getting scarce. The firing was less frequent, though the watch was as close as ever, and twice a Winchester had sounded a signal of distress. All knew that a response must come soon; and come it did. A picket, watching the river road, saw young Jasper's horse coming along the dark bushes far up the river, and brought the news to the group standing behind old Sam's cabin. The gray galloped into sight, and, skirting the woods, came straight for the town—with a woman on his back. The stirrup of a man's saddle dangled on one side, and the woman's bonnet had fallen from her head. Some one challenged her.

"Stop, I tell ye! Don't ye go near that court-house! Stop, I tell ye! I'll shoot! Stop!"

Rome ran from the cabin with a revolver in each hand. A drunken mountaineer was raising a Winchester to his shoulder, and, springing from the back of the gray at the court-house steps, was Martha Lewallen.

"I'll kill the fust man that lifts his finger to hurt the gal," Rome said, knocking the drunken man's gun in the air. "We hain't fightin' women!"

It was too late to oppose her, and the crowd

stood helplessly watching. No one dared approach, so, shielding with her body the space of
the opening door, she threw the sack of food
within. Then she stood a moment talking and,
turning, climbed to her saddle. The gray was
spotted with foam, and showed the red of his
nostrils with every breath as, with face flushed
and eyes straight before her, she rode slowly
toward the crowd. What was she about?
Rome stood rigid, his forgotten pistols hanging
at each side; the mouth of the drunken mountaineer was open with stupid wonder; the rest
fell apart as she came around the corner of the
cabin and, through the space given, rode slowly,
her skirt almost brushing Rome, looking neither
to the right nor to the left; and when she had
gone quite through them all, she wheeled and
rode, still slowly, through the open fields toward the woods which sheltered the Lewallens,
while the crowd stood in bewildered silence
looking after her. Yells of laughter came from
the old court-house. Some of the Stetsons
laughed, too; some swore, a few grumbled; but
there was not one who was not stirred by the
superb daring of the girl, though she had used
it only to show her contempt.

"Rome, you're a fool; though, fer a fac', we
can't shoot a woman; 'n' anyways I ruther shoot
her than the hoss. But lemme tell ye, thar was

" 'We bain't fightin' women!' "

more'n sump'n to eat in that bag! They air up to some dodge."

Rufe Stetson had watched the incident through a port-hole of the cabin, and his tone was at once jesting and anxious.

"That grub won't last more'n one day, I reckon," said the drunken mountaineer. "We'll watch out fer the gal nex' time. We're boun' to git 'em one time or t'other."

"She rid through us to find out how many of us wasn't dead drunk," said Steve Marcum, still watching the girl as she rode on, toward the woods; " 'n' I'm a-thinkin' they'll be down on us purty soon now, 'n' I reckon we'll have to run fer it. Look thar boys! "

The girl had stopped at the edge of the woods; facing the town, she waved her bonnet high above her head.

" Well, whut in the ——! " he said, with slow emphasis, and then he leaped from the door with a yell. The bonnet was a signal to the beleaguered Lewallens. The rear door of the court-house had been quietly opened, and the prisoners were out in a body and scrambling over the fence before the pickets could give an alarm. The sudden yells, the crack of Winchesters, startled even the revellers; and all who could, headed by Rome and Steve Marcum, sprang into the square, and started in pursuit. But the Lewallens had got far ahead, and were running in zigzag lines to dodge the balls flying after them. Half-way to the woods was a gully of red clay, and into this the fleetest leaped, and turned instantly to cover their comrades. The Winchesters began to rattle from the woods, and the bullets came like rain from everywhere.

"T-h-up! T-h-up! T-h-up!" there were three of them—the peculiar soft, dull messages of hot lead to living flesh. A Stetson went down; another stumbled; Rufe Stetson, climbing the fence, caught at his breast with an oath, and fell back. Rome and Steve dropped for safety to the ground. Every other Stetson turned in a panic, and every Lewallen in the gully leaped from it, and ran under the Lewallen fire for shelter in the woods. The escape was over.

"That was a purty neat trick," said Steve, wiping a red streak from his cheek. "Nex' time she tries that, she'll git herself into trouble."

At nightfall the wounded leader and the dead one were carried up the mountain, each to his home; and there was mourning far into the night on one bank of the Cumberland, and, serious though Rufe Stetson's wound was, exultation on the other. But in it Rome could take but little part. There had been no fault to find with him in the fight. But a reaction had set in when he saw the girl flash in the moonlight past the sights of his Winchester, and her face that day had again loosed within him a flood of feeling that drove the lust for revenge from his veins. Even now, while he sat in his own cabin, his thoughts were across the river where Martha, broken at last, sat at her death vigils. He knew what her daring ride that day had cost her, with old Jasper dead out there in the woods; and as she passed him he had grown suddenly humbled, shamed. He grew heart-sick now as he thought of it all; and the sight of his mother on her bed in the corner, close to death as she was, filled him with bitterness. There was no help for him. He was alone now, pitted against young Jasper alone. On one bed lay his uncle—nigh to death. There was the grim figure in the corner, the implacable spirit of hate and revenge. His rifle was against the wall. If there was any joy for him in old Jasper's death, it was that his hand had not caused it, and yet—God help him!— there was the other cross, the other oath.

XII

THE star and the crescent were swinging above Wolf's Head, and in the dark hour that breaks into dawn a cavalcade of Lewallens forded the Cumberland, and galloped along the Stetson shore. At the head rode young Jasper, and Crump the spy.

Swift changes had followed the court-house fight. In spite of the death of Rufe Stetson from his wound, and several other Stetsons from ambush, the Lewallens had lost ground. Old Jasper's store had fallen into the hands of creditors —" furriners "—for debts, and it was said his homestead must follow. In a private war a leader must be more than leader. He must feed and often clothe his followers, and young Jasper had not the means to carry on the feud. The famine had made corn dear. He could feed neither man nor horse, and the hired feudsmen fell away, leaving the Lewallens and the Braytons and their close kin to battle alone. So Jasper avoided open combat and resorted to ambush and surprise; and, knowing in some way every move made by the Stetsons, with great daring

and success. It was whispered, too, that he no
longer cared who owned what he might want for
himself. Several dark deeds were traced to him.
In a little while he was a terror to good citizens,
and finally old Gabe asked aid of the Governor.
Soldiers from the settlements were looked for any
day, and both factions knew it. At the least this
would delay the war, and young Jasper had got
ready for a last fight, which was close at hand.

Half a mile on the riders swerved into a
wooded slope. There they hid their horses in
the brush, and climbed the spur stealthily. The
naked woods showed the cup-like shape of the
mountains there—a basin from which radiated
upward wooded ravines, edged with ribs of rock.
In this basin the Stetsons were encamped. The
smoke of a fire was visible in the dim morning
light, and the Lewallens scattered to surround
the camp, but the effort was vain. A picket saw
the creeping figures; his gun echoed a warning
from rock to rock, and with yells the Lewallens
ran forward. Rome sprang from his sleep near
the fire, bareheaded, rifle in hand, his body plain
against a huge rock, and the bullets hissed and
spat about him as he leaped this way and that,
firing as he sprang, and shouting for his men.
Steve Marcum alone answered. Some, startled
from sleep, had fled in a panic; some had run
deeper into the woods for shelter. And bidding

Steve save himself, Rome turned up the mountain, running from tree to tree, and dropped unhurt behind a fallen chestnut. Other Stetsons, too, had turned, and answering bullets began to whistle to the enemy, but they were widely separated and ignorant of one another's position, and the Lewallens drove them one by one to new hiding-places, scattering them more. To his right Rome saw Steve Marcum speed like a shadow up through a little open space, but he feared to move, for several Lewallens had recognized him, and were watching him alone. He could not even fire; at the least exposure there was a chorus of bullets about his ears. In a moment they began to come obliquely from each side —the Lewallens were getting around him. In a moment more death was sure there, and once again he darted up the mountain. The bullets sang after him like maddened bees. He felt one cut his hat and another sting his left arm, but he raced up, up, till the firing grew fainter as he climbed, and ceased an instant altogether. Then, still farther below, came a sudden crash of reports. Stetsons were pursuing the men who were after him, but he could not join them. The Lewallens were scattered everywhere between him and his own man, and a descent might lead him to the muzzle of an enemy's Winchester. So he climbed over a ledge of rock and lay there, peeping through a crevice between two bowlders, gaining his breath. The firing was far below him now, and was sharp. Evidently his pursuers were too busy defending themselves to think further of him, and he began to plan how he should get back to his friends. But he kept hidden, and, searching the cliffs below him for a sheltered descent, he saw something like a slouched hat just over a log, scarcely fifty feet below him. Presently the hat was lifted a few inches; a figure rose cautiously and climbed toward the ledge, shielding itself behind rock and tree. Very quietly Rome crawled back to the face of the cliff behind him, and crouched behind a rock with his cocked rifle across his knees. The man must climb over the ledge; there would be a bare, level floor of rock between them—the Lewallen would be at his mercy—and Rome, with straining eyes, waited. There was a footfall on the other side of the ledge; a soft clink of metal against stone. The Lewallen was climbing slowly—slowly. Rome could hear his heavy breathing. A grimy hand slipped over the sharp comb of the ledge; another appeared, clinched about a Winchester—then the slouched hat, and under it the dark, crafty face of young Jasper. Rome sat like the stone before him, with a half-smile on his lips. Jasper peered about with the sly caution of a fox, and his face grew puzzled and chagrined as he looked at the cliffs above him.

" Stop thar ! "

He was drawing himself over the ledge, and the low, stern voice startled him, as a knife might have done, thrust suddenly from the empty air at his breast. Rome rose upright against the cliff, with his resolute face against the stock of a Winchester.

" Drap that gun ! "

The order was given along Stetson's barrel, and the weapon was dropped, the steel ringing on the stone floor. Rome lowered his gun to the hollow of his arm, and the two young leaders faced each other for the first time in the life of either.

" Seem kinder s'prised to see me," said the Stetson, grimly. " Hev ye got a pistol ? "

Young Jasper glared at him in helpless ferocity.

" Naw ! "

" Knife ? "

He drew a long-bladed penknife from his pocket, and tossed it at Rome's feet.

" Jes' move over thar, will ye ? "

The Lewallen took his stand against the cliff. Rome picked up the fallen rifle and leaned it against the ledge.

" Now, Jas Lewallen, thar's nobody left in

this leetle trouble 'cept you 'n' me, 'n' ef one of us was dead, I reckon t'other could live hyeh, 'n' thar'd be peace in these mount'ins. I thought o' that when I had ye at the eend o' this Winchester. I reckon you would 'a' shot me dead ef I had poked my head over a rock as keerless as you." That is just what he would have done, and Jasper did not answer. "I've swore to kill ye, too," added Rome, tapping his gun; "I've got a cross fer ye hyeh."

The Lewallen was no coward. Outcry or resistance was useless. The Stetson meant to taunt him, to make death more bitter; for Jasper expected death, and he sullenly waited for it against the cliff.

"You've been banterin' me a long time now, 'lowin' as how ye air the better man o' the two; 'n' I've got a notion o' givin' ye a chance to prove yer tall talk. Hit's not *our* way to kill a man in cold blood, 'n' I don't want to kill ye anyways ef I kin he'p it. Seem s'prised ag'in. Reckon ye don't believe me? I don't wonder when I think o' my own dad, 'n' all the meanness yo' folks have done mine; but I've got a good reason fer not killin' ye—ef I kin he'p it. Y'u don't know what it is, 'n' y'u'll never know; but I'll give yer a chance now fer yer life ef y'u'll sw'ar on a stack o' Bibles as high as that tree thar that y'u'll leave these mount'ins ef I whoops ye, 'n' nuver come back ag'in as long as you live. *I'll* leave, ef ye whoops me. Now whut do ye say? Will ye sw'ar?"

" I reckon I will, seein' as I've got to," was the surly answer. But Jasper's face was dark with suspicion, and Rome studied it keenly. The Lewallens once had been men whose word was good, but he did not like Jasper's look.

" I reckon I'll trust ye," he said, at last, more through confidence in his own strength than faith in his enemy; foɪ Jasper whipped would be as much at his mercy as he was now. So Rome threw off his coat, and began winding his home-spun suspenders about his waist. Watching him closely, Jasper did the same.

The firing below had ceased. A flock of mountain vultures were sailing in great circles over the thick woods. Two eagles swept straight from the rim of the sun above Wolf's Head, beating over a turbulent sea of mist for the cliffs, scarcely fifty yards above the ledge, where a pine-tree grew between two rocks. At the instant of lighting, they wheeled away, each with a warning scream to the other. A figure lying flat behind the pine had frightened them, and now a face peeped to one side, flushed with eagerness over the coming fight. Both were ready now, and the Lewallen grew suddenly white as Rome turned again and reached down for the guns.

" I reckon I'll put 'em a leetle furder out o'
the way," he said, kicking the knife over the
cliff; and, standing on a stone, he thrust them
into a crevice high above his head.

" Now, Jas, we'll fight this gredge out, as our
grandads have done afore us."

Lewallen and Stetson were man to man at last.
Suspicion was gone now, and a short, brutal
laugh came from the cliff.

" I'll fight ye! Oh, by *God*, I'll fight ye! "

The ring of the voice struck an answering
gleam from Rome's gray eyes, and the two
sprang for each other. It was like the struggle
of primeval men who had not yet learned even
the use of clubs. For an instant both stood close,
like two wild beasts crouched for a spring, and
circling about to get at each other's throats, with
mouths set, eyes watching eyes, and hands twitch-
ing nervously. Young Jasper leaped first, and
the Stetson, wary of closing with him, shrank
back. There were a few quick, heavy blows,
and the Lewallen was beaten away with blood at
his lips. Then each knew the advantage of the
other. The Stetson's reach was longer; the Lewallen was shorter and heavier, and again he
closed in. Again Rome sent out his long arm.
A turn of Jasper's head let the heavy fist pass
over his shoulder. The force of the blow drove
Rome forward; the two clinched, and Jasper's

arms tightened about the Stetson's waist. With
a quick gasp for breath Rome loosed his hold,
and, bending his enemy's head back with one
hand, rained blow after blow in his face with
the other. One terrible stroke on the jaw, and
Jasper's arms were loosed; the two fell apart,
the one stunned, the other breathless. One dazed
moment only, and for a third time the Lewallen
came on. Rome had been fighting a man; now
he faced a demon. Jasper's brows stood out like
bristles, and the eyes under them were red and
fierce like a mad bull's. Again Rome's blows
fell, but again the Lewallen reached him, and
this time he got his face under the Stetson's chin,
and the heavy fist fell upon the back of his head,
and upon his neck, as upon wood and leather.
Again Rome had to gasp for breath, and again
the two were fiercely locked—their corded arms
as tense as serpents. Around and around they
whirled, straining, tripping, breaking the silence
only with deep, quick breaths and the stamping
of feet, Jasper firm on the rock, and Rome's
agility saving him from being lifted in the air
and tossed from the cliff. There was no pause
for rest. It was a struggle to the end, and a
quick one; and under stress of excitement the
figure at the pine-tree had risen to his knees—
jumping even to his feet in plain view, when the
short, strong arms of the Lewallen began at last

to draw Rome closer still, and to bend him backward. The Stetson was giving way at last. The Lewallen's vindictive face grew blacker, and his white teeth showed between his snarling lips as he fastened one leg behind his enemy's, and, with chin against his shoulder, bent him slowly, slowly back. The two breathed in short, painful gasps; their swollen muscles trembled under the strain as with ague. Back — back — the Stetson was falling; he seemed almost down, when—the trick is an old one—whirling with the quickness of light, he fell heavily on his opponent, and caught him by the throat with both hands.

" 'Nough? " he asked, hoarsely. It was the first word uttered.

The only answer was a fierce struggle. Rome felt the Lewallen's teeth sinking in his arm, and his fingers tightened like twisting steel, till Jasper caught his breath as though strangling to death.

" 'Nough? " asked the hoarse voice again.

No answer; tighter clinched the fingers. The Lewallen shook his head feebly; his purple face paled suddenly as Rome loosed his hold, and his lips moved in a whisper.

" 'Nough! "

Rome rose dizzily to one knee. Jasper turned, gasping, and lay with his face to the rock. For a while both were quiet, Rome, panting with open mouth and white with exhaustion, looking down now and then at the Lewallen, whose face was turned away with shame.

The sun was blazing above Wolf's Head now, and the stillness about them lay unbroken on the woods below.

" I've whooped ye, Jas," Rome said, at last; " I've whooped ye in a fa'r fight, 'n' I've got nothin' now to say 'bout yer tall talk, 'n' I reckon you hevn't nuther. Now, hit's understood, hain't it, that y'u'll leave these mount'ins?

" Y'u kin go West," he continued, as the Lewallen did not answer. " Uncle Rufe used to say thar's a good deal to do out thar, 'n' nobody axes questions. Thar's nobody left hyeh but you 'n' me, but these mount'ins was never big 'noug̍. fer one Lewallen 'n' one Stetson, 'n' you've got to go. I reckon ye won't believe me, but I'm glad I didn't hev to kill ye. But you've promised to go, now, 'n' I'll take yer word fer it."
He turned his face, and the Lewallen, knowing it from the sound of his voice, sprang to his feet.

" Oh ——! "

A wild curse burst from Rome's lips, and both leaped for the guns. The Lewallen had the start of a few feet, and Rome, lamed in the fight, stumbled and fell. Before he could rise Jasper had whirled, with one of the Winchesters above his head and his face aflame with fury. Asking

210

no mercy, Rome hid his face with one arm and waited, stricken faint all at once, and numb. One report struck his ears, muffled, whip-like. A dull wonder came to him that the Lewallen could have missed at such close range, and he waited for another. Some one shouted—a shrill halloo. A loud laugh followed; a light seemed breaking before Rome's eyes, and he lifted his head. Jasper was on his face again, motionless; and Steve Marcum's tall figure was climbing over a bowlder toward him.

" That was the best fight I've seed in my time, by *God,*" he said, coolly, " 'n', Rome, y'u air the biggest fool this side o' the settlements, I reckon. I had dead aim on him, 'n' I was jest a-thinkin' hit was a purty good thing fer you that old long-nosed Jim Stover chased me up hyeh, when, damn me, ef that boy up thar didn't let his ole gun loose. I'd a-got Jas myself ef he hadn't been so all-fired quick o' trigger."

Up at the root of the pine-tree Isom stood motionless, with his long rifle in one hand and a little cloud of smoke breaking above his white face. When Rome looked up he started down without a word. Steve swung himself over the ledge.

" I heerd the shootin'," said the boy, " up thar at the cave, 'n' I couldn't stay thar. I knowed ye could whoop him, Rome, 'n' I seed Steve, too,

but I was afeard——" Then he saw the body.
His tongue stopped, his face shrivelled, and
Steve, hanging with one hand to the ledge,
watched him curiously.

" Rome," said the boy, in a quick whisper,
" is he daid? "

" Come on! " said Steve, roughly. " They'll
be up hyeh atter us in a minute. Leave Jas's
gun thar, 'n' send that boy back home."

That day the troops came—young Blue Grass
Kentuckians. That night, within the circle of
their camp-fires, a last defiance was cast in the
teeth of law and order. Flames rose within the
old court-house, and before midnight the moonlight fell on four black walls. That night, too,
the news of young Jasper's fate was carried to
the death-bed of Rome's mother, and before day
the old woman passed in peace. That day Stetsons and Lewallens disbanded. The Lewallens
had no leader; the Stetsons, no enemies to fight.
Some hid, some left the mountains, some gave
themselves up for trial. Upon Rome Stetson
the burden fell. Against him the law was set.
A price was put on his head, his house was
burned—a last act of Lewallen hate—and Rome
was homeless, the last of his race, and an out-
law.

XIII

WITH the start of a few hours and the sympathy of his people one mountaineer can defy the army of the United States; and the mountaineers usually laugh when they hear troops are coming. For the time they stop fighting and hide in the woods; and when the soldiers are gone, they come out again, and begin anew their little pleasantries. But the soldiers can protect the judge on his bench and the county-seat in time of court, and for these purposes they serve well.

The search for Rome Stetson, then, was useless. His friends would aid him; his enemies feared to betray him. So the soldiers marched away one morning, and took their prisoners for safe-keeping in the Blue Grass, until court should open at Hazlan.

Meantime, spring came and deepened—the mountain spring. The berries of the wintergreen grew scarce, and Rome Stetson, " hiding out," as the phrase is, had to seek them on the northern face of the mountains. The moss on the naked winter trees brightened in color, and along

the river, where willows drooped, ran faint lines
of green. The trailing arbutus gave out delicate
pink blossoms, and the south wind blew apart
the petals of the anemone. Soon violets unfold-
ed above the dead leaves; azaleas swung their
yellow trumpets through the undergrowth; overhead, the dogwood tossed its snow-flakes in gusts
through the green and gold of new leaves and
sunlight; and higher still waved the poplar
blooms, with honey ready on every crimson heart
for the bees. Down in the valley Rome Stetson
could see about every little cabin pink clouds and
white clouds of peach and of apple blossoms.
Amid the ferns about him shade-loving trilliums
showed their many-hued faces, and every opening was thickly peopled with larkspur seeking
the sun. The giant magnolia and the umbrella-
tree spread their great creamy flowers; the laurel
shook out myriads of pink and white bells, and
the queen of mountain flowers was stirring from
sleep in the buds of the rhododendron.

With the spring new forces pulsed the mountain air. The spirit of the times reached even
Hazlan. A railroad was coming up the river,
so the rumor was. When winter broke, survey-
ors had appeared; after them, mining experts
and purchasers of land. New ways of bread-
making were open to all, and the feudsman began to see that he could make food and clothes

more easily and with less danger than by sleeping with his rifle in the woods, and by fighting men who had done him no harm. Many were tired of fighting; many, forced into the feud, had fought unwillingly. Others had sold their farms and wild lands, and were moving toward the Blue Grass or westward. The desperadoes of each faction had fled the law or were in its clutches. The last Lewallen was dead; the last Stetson was hidden away in the mountains. There were left Marcums and Braytons, but only those who felt safest from indictment; in these a spirit of hostility would live for years, and, roused by passion or by drink, would do murder now on one side of the Cumberland and now on the other; but the Stetson-Lewallen feud, old Gabe believed, was at an end at last.

All these things the miller told Rome Stetson, who well knew what they meant. He was safe enough from the law while the people took no part in his capture, but he grew apprehensive when he learned of the changes going on in the valley. None but old Gabe knew where he was, to be sure, but with his own enemies to guide the soldiers he could not hope to remain hidden long. Still, with that love of the mountains characteristic of all races born among them, he clung to his own land. He would rather stay where he was the space of a year and die, he told old Gabe

passionately, than live to old age in another
State.

But there was another motive, and he did not
hide it. On the other side he had one enemy
left—the last, too, of her race—who was more
to him than his own dead kindred, who hated
him, who placed at his door all her sorrows.
For her he was living like a wolf in a cave, and
old Gabe knew it. Her—he would not leave.

"I tell ye, Rome, you've *got* to go. Thar's
no use talkin'. Court comes the fust Monday
in June. The soldiers ull be hyeh. Hit won't
be safe. Thar's some that s'picions I know whar
ye air now, 'n' they'll be spyin', 'n' mebbe hit'll
git me into trouble, too, aidin' 'n' abettin' a man
to git away who air boun' to the law."

The two were sitting on the earthen floor of
the cave before a little fire, and Rome, with his
hands about his knees and his brows knitted, was
staring into the yellow blaze. His unshorn hair
fell to his shoulders; his face was pale from in-
sufficient food and exercise, and tense with a look
that was at once caged and defiant.

"Uncle Gabe," he asked, quietly, for the old
man's tone was a little querulous, "air ye sorry
ye holped me? Do ye blame me fer whut I've
done?"

"No," said the old miller, answering both
questions; "I don't. I believe whut ye tol' me.

Though, even ef ye had 'a' done it, I don't know as I'd blame ye, seein' that it was a fa'r fight. I don't doubt he was doin' his best to kill you."

Rome turned quickly, his face puzzled and darkening.

" Uncle Gabe, whut air you drivin' at? " The old man spat into the fire, and shifted his position uneasily, as Rome's hand caught his knee.

" Well, ef I have to tell ye, I s'pose I must. Thar's been nothin' pertickler ag'in ye so fer, 'cept fer breakin' that confederatin' statute 'bout bandin' fightin' men together; 'n' nobody was very anxious to git hol' o' ye jes fer that, but now "—the old man stopped a moment, for Rome's eyes were kindling—" they say that ye killed Jas Lewallen, 'n' that ye air a murderer; 'n' hit air powerful strange how all of a suddint folks seem to be gittin' down on a man as kills his fellow-creetur; 'n' now they means to hunt ye till they ketch ye."

It was all out now, and the old man was relieved. Rome rose to his feet, and in sheer agony of spirit paced the floor.

" I tol' ye, Uncle Gabe, that I didn't kill him."

" So ye did, 'n' I believe ye. But a feller seed you 'n' Steve comin' from the place whar Jas was found dead, 'n' whar the dirt 'n' rock was

217

throwed about as by two bucks in spring-time.. Steve says he didn't do it, 'n' he wouldn't say you didn't. Looks to me like Steve did the killin', 'n' was lyin' a leetle. He hain't goin' to confess hit to save your neck; 'n' he can't no way, fer he hev lit out o' these mount'ins—long ago."

If Steve was out of danger, suspicion could not harm him, and Rome said nothing.

" Isom's got the lingerin' fever ag'in, 'n' he's out'n his head. He's ravin' 'bout that fight. Looks like ye tol' him 'bout it. He says, ' Don't tell Uncle Gabe'; 'n' he keeps sayin' it. Hit'll 'most kill him ef you go 'way; but _he_ wants ye to git out o' the mount'ins; 'n', Rome, you've got to go."

"Who was it, Uncle Gabe, that seed me 'n' Steve comin' 'way from thar?"

" He air the same feller who hev been spyin' ye all the time this war's been goin' on; hit's that dried-faced, snaky Eli Crump, who ye knocked down 'n' choked up in Hazlan one day fer sayin' something ag'in Isom."

" I knowed it—I knowed it—oh, ef I could git my fingers roun' his throat once more—jes once more—I'd be 'mos' ready to die."

He stretched out his hands as he strode back and forth, with his fingers crooked like talons; his shadow leaped from wall to wall, and his voice, filling the cave, was, for the moment, scarcely human. The old man waited till the paroxysm was over and Rome had again sunk before the fire.

" Hit 'u'd do no good, Rome," he said, rising to go. " You've got enough on ye now, without the sin o' takin' his life. You better make up yer mind to leave the mount'ins now right 'way. You're a-gittin' no more'n half-human, livin' up hyeh like a catamount. I don't see how ye kin stand it. Thar's no hope o' things blowin' over, boy, 'n' givin' ye a chance o' comin' out ag'in, as yer dad and yer grandad usen to do afore ye. The citizens air gittin' tired o' these wars. They keeps out the furriners who makes roads 'n' buys lands; they air ag'in' the law, ag'in' religion, ag'in' yo' pocket, 'n' ag'in' mine. Lots o' folks hev been ag'in' all this fightin' fer a long time, but they was too skeery to say so. They air talkin' mighty big now, seein' they kin git soldiers hyeh to pertect 'em. So ye mought as well give up the idea o' staying hyeh, 'less'n ye want to give yourself up to the law."

The two stepped from the cave, and passed through the rhododendrons till they stood on the cliff overlooking the valley. The rich light lay like a golden mist between the mountains, and through it, far down, the river moaned like the wind of a coming storm.

" Did ye tell the gal whut I tol' ye? "

" Yes, Rome; hit wasn't no use. She says Steve's word's as good as yourn; 'n' she knowed about the crosses. Folks say she swore awful ag'in' ye at young Jas's burial, 'lowin' that she'd hunt ye down herse'f, ef the soldiers didn't ketch ye. I hain't seed her sence she got sick; 'pears like ever'body's sick. Mebbe she's a leetle settled down now—no tellin'. No use foolin' with her, Rome. You git away from hyeh. Don't you worry 'bout Isom—I'll take keer o' him, 'n' when he gits well, he'll want to come atter ye, 'n' I'll let him go. He couldn't live hyeh without you. But y'u must git away, Rome, 'n' git away mighty quick."

With hands clasped behind him, Rome stood and watched the bent figure slowly pick its way around the stony cliff.

" I reckon I've got to go. She's ag'in' me; they're all ag'in' me. I reckon I've jes *got* to go. Somehow, I've been kinder hopin'——" He closed his lips to check the groan that rose to them, and turned again into the gloom behind him.

XIV

JUNE came. The wild rose swayed above its
image along every little shadowed stream,
and the scent of wild gra⁊es was sweet in the air
and as vagrant as a bluebird's note in autumn.
The rhododendrons burst into beauty, making
gray ridge and gray cliff blossom with purple,
hedging streams with snowy clusters and shining
leaves, and lighting up dark coverts in the woods
as with white stars. The leaves were full, wood-
thrushes sang, and bees droned like unseen running water in the woods.

With June came circuit court once more—and
the soldiers. Faint music pierced the dreamy
chant of the river one morning as Rome lay on a
bowlder in the summer sun; and he watched the
guns flashing like another stream along the water, and then looked again to the Lewallen cabin.
Never, morning, noon, or night, when he came
from the rhododendrons, or when they closed
about him, did he fail to turn his eyes that way.
Often he would see a bright speck moving about
the dim lines of the cabin, and he would scarcely
breathe while he watched it, so easily would it

disappear. Always he had thought it was Martha, and now he knew it was, for the old miller had told him more of the girl, and had wrung his heart with pity. She had been ill a long while. The " furriners " had seized old Jasper's cabin and land. The girl was homeless, and she did not know it, for no one had the heart to tell her. She was living with the Braytons; and every day she went to the cabin, " moonin' 'n' sorrowin' aroun'," as old Gabe said; and she was much changed.

Once more the miller came—for the last time, he said, firmly. Crump had trailed him, and had learned where Rome was. The search would begin next day—perhaps that very night—and Crump would guide the soldiers. Now he must go, and go quickly. The boy, too, sent word that unless Rome went, he would have something to tell. Old Gabe saw no significance in the message; but he had promised to deliver it, and he did. Rome wavered then; Steve and himself gone, no suspicion would fall on the lad. If he were caught, the boy might confess. With silence Rome gave assent, and the two parted in an apathy that was like heartlessness. Only old Gabe's shrunken breast heaved with something more than weariness of descent, and Rome stood watching him a long time before he turned back to the cave that had sheltered him from his enemies among beasts and men. In a moment he came out for the last time, and turned the opposite way. Climbing about the spur, he made for the path that led down to the river. When he reached it he glanced at the sun, and stopped in indecision. Straight above him was a knoll, massed with rhododendrons, the flashing leaves of which made it like a great sea-wave in the slanting sun, while the blooms broke slowly down over it like foam. Above this was a gray sepulchre of dead, standing trees, more gaunt and spectre-like than ever, with the rich life of summer about it. Higher still were a dark belt of stunted firs and the sandstone ledge, and above these—home. He was risking his liberty, his life. Any clump of bushes might bristle suddenly with Winchesters. If the soldiers sought for him at the cave they would at the same time guard the mountain paths; they would guard, too, the Stetson cabin. But no matter—the sun was still high, and he turned up the steep. The ledge passed, he stopped with a curse at his lips and the pain of a knife-thrust at his heart. A heap of blackened stones and ashes was before him. The wild mountain-grass was growing up about it. The bee-gums were overturned and rifled. The garden was a tangled mass of weeds. The graves in the little family burying-ground were unprotected, the fence was gone, and no boards marked the last two ragged mounds. Old Gabe had never told him. He, too, like Martha, was homeless, and the old miller had been kind to him, as the girl's kinspeople had been to her.

For a long while he sat on the remnant of the burned and broken fence, and once more the old tide of bitterness rose within him and ebbed away. There were none left to hate, to wreak vengeance on. It was hard to leave the ruins as they were; and yet he would rather leave weeds and ashes than, like Martha, have some day to know that his home was in the hands of a stranger. When he thought of the girl he grew calmer; his own sorrows gave way to the thought of hers; and half from habit he raised his face to look across the river. Two eagles swept from a dark ravine under the shelf of rock where he had fought young Jasper, and made for a sunlighted peak on the other shore. From them his gaze fell to Wolf's Head and to the cabin beneath, and a name passed his lips in a whisper.

Then he took the path to the river, and he found the canoe where old Gabe had hidden it. Before the young moon rose he pushed into the stream and drifted with the current. At the mouth of the creek that ran over old Gabe's water-wheel he turned the prow to the Lewallen shore.

"Not yit! Not yit!" he said.

224

XV

THAT night Rome passed in the woods, with his rifle, in a bed of leaves. Before daybreak he had built a fire in a deep ravine to cook his breakfast, and had scattered the embers that the smoke should give no sign. The sun was high when he crept cautiously in sight of the Lewallen cabin. It was much like his own home on the other shore, except that the house, closed and desolate, was standing, and the bees were busy. At the corner of the kitchen a rusty axe was sticking in a half-cut piece of timber, and on the porch was a heap of kindling and fire wood—the last work old Jasper and his son had ever done. In the Lewallens' garden, also, two graves were fresh; and the spirit of neglect and ruin overhung the place.

All the morning he waited in the edge of the laurel, peering down the path, watching the clouds race with their shadows over the mountains, or pacing to and fro in his covert of leaves and flowers. He began to fear at last that she was not coming, that she was ill, and once he started down the mountain toward Steve Brayton's cabin. The swift descent brought him to his senses, and he stopped half-way, and climbed back again to his hiding-place. What he was doing, what he meant to do, he hardly knew. Mid-day passed; the sun fell toward the mountains, and once more came the fierce impulse to see her, even though he must stalk into the Brayton cabin. Again, half-crazed, he started impetuously through the brush, and shrank back, and stood quiet. A little noise down the path had reached his ear. In a moment he could hear slow foot-falls, and the figure of the girl parted the pink-and-white laurel blossoms, which fell in a shower about her when she brushed through them. She passed quite near him, walking slowly, and stopped for a moment to rest against a pillar of the porch. She was very pale; her face was traced deep with suffering, and she was, as old Gabe said, much changed. Then she went on toward the garden, stepping with an effort over the low fence, and leaned as if weak and tired against the apple-tree, the boughs of which shaded the two graves at her feet. For a few moments she stood there, listless, and Rome watched her with hungry eyes, at a loss what to do. She moved presently, and walked quite around the graves without looking at them; then came back past him, and, seating herself in the porch, turned her face to the river. The sun lighted her hair, and in the sunken, upturned eyes Rome saw the shimmer of tears.

"Marthy!" He couldn't help it—the thick, low cry broke like a groan from his lips, and the girl was on her feet, facing him. She did not know the voice, nor the shaggy, half-wild figure in the shade of the laurel; and she started back as if to run; but seeing that the man did not mean to harm her, she stopped, looking for a moment with wonder and even with quick pity at the hunted face with its white appeal. Then a sudden spasm caught her throat, and left her body rigid, her hands shut, and her eyes dry and hard—she knew him. A slow pallor drove the flush of surprise from her face, and her lips moved once, but there was not even a whisper from them. Rome raised one hand before his face, as though to ward off something. "Don't look at me that way, Marthy—my God, don't! I didn't kill him. I sw'ar it! I give him a chance fer his life. I know, I know—Steve says he didn't. Thar was only us two. Hit looks ag'in' me; but I hain't killed one nur t'other. I let 'em both go. Y'u don't believe me?" He went swiftly toward her, his gun outstretched. "Hyeh, gal! I heerd ye swore ag'in' me out thar in the gyarden—'lowin' that you was goin' to hunt me down yerself if the soldiers didn't. Hyeh's yer chance!"

The girl shrank away from him, too startled to take the weapon; and he leaned it against her, and stood away, with his hands behind him.

"Kill me ef ye think I'm a-lyin' to ye," he said. "Y'u kin git even with me now. But I want to tell ye fust "—the girl had caught the muzzle of the gun convulsively, and was bending over it, her eyes burning, her face inscrutable— "hit was a fa'r fight betwixt us, 'n' I whooped him. He got his gun then, 'n' would 'a' killed me ag'in' his oath ef he hadn't been shot fust. Hit's so, too, 'bout the crosses. I made 'em; they're right thar on that gun; but whut could I do with mam a-standin' right thar with the gun 'n' Uncle Rufe a-tellin' 'bout my own dad layin' in his blood, 'n' Isom 'n' the boys lookin' on! But I went ag'in' my oath; I gave him his life when I had the right to take it. I could 'a' killed yer dad once, 'n' I had the right to kill him, too, fer killin' mine; but I let him go, 'n' I reckon I done that fer ye, too. 'Pears like I hain't done nothin' sence I seed ye over thar in the mill that day that wasn't done fer ye. Somehow ye put me dead ag'in' my own kin, 'n' tuk away all my hate ag'in' yourn. I couldn't fight fer thinkin' I was fightin' you, 'n' when I seed ye comin' through the bushes jes now, so white 'n' sickly-like, I couldn't hardly git breath, a-thinkin' I was the cause of all yer misery. That's all!" He stretched out his arms. "Shoot, gal, ef ye don't believe me. I'd jes as lieve die, ef ye thinks I'm lyin' to yė, 'n' ef ye hates me fer whut I hain't done."

The gun had fallen to the earth. The girl, trembling at the knees, sank to her seat on the porch, and, folding her arms against the pillar, pressed her forehead against them, her face unseen. Rome stooped to pick up the weapon.

"I'm goin' 'way now," he went on, slowly, after a little pause, "but I couldn't leave hyeh without seein' you. I wanted ye to know the truth, 'n' I 'lowed y'u'd believe me ef I tol' ye myself. I've been a-waitin' thar in the lorrel fer ye sence mornin'. Uncle Gabe tol' me ye come hyeh ever' day. He says I've got to go. I've been hopin' I mought come out o' the bushes some day. But Uncle Gabe says ever'body's ag'in' me more'n ever, 'n' that the soldiers mean to ketch me. The gov'ner out thar in the settlements says as how he'll give five hundred dollars fer me, livin' or dead. He'll nuver git me livin' —I've swore that—'n' as I hev done nothin' sech as folks on both sides hev done who air walkin' roun' free, I hain't goin' to give up. Hit's purty hard to leave these mount'ins. Reckon I'll nuver see 'em ag'in. Been livin' like a catamount over thar on the knob. I could jes see you over hyeh, 'n' I reckon I hain't done much 'cept lay over thar on a rock 'n' watch ye movin' round. Hit's mighty good to feel that ye believe me, 'n' I want ye to know that I been stayin' over thar fer nothin' on earth but jes to see you ag'in; 'n' I want ye to know that I was a-sorrowin' fer ye when y'u was sick, 'n' a-pinin' to see ye, 'n' a-hopin' some day y'u mought kinder git over yer hate fer me." He had been talking with low tenderness, half to himself, and with his face to the river, and he did not see the girl's tears falling to the porch. Her sorrow gave way in a great sob now, and he turned with sharp remorse, and stood quite near her.

"Don't cry, Marthy," he said. "God knows hit's hard to think I've brought all this on ye when I'd give all these mount'ins to save ye from it. Whut d' ye say? Don't cry."

The girl was trying to speak at last, and Rome bent over to catch the words.

"I hain't cryin' fer myself," she said, faintly, and then she said no more; but the first smile that had passed over Rome's face for many a day passed then, and he put out one big hand, and let it rest on the heap of lustrous hair.

"Marthy, I hate to go 'way, leavin' ye hyeh with nobody to take keer o' ye. You're all alone

230

hyeh in the mount'ins; I'm all alone; 'n' I reckon
I'll be all alone wharever I go, ef you stay hyeh.
I got a boat down thar on the river, 'n' I'm goin'
out West whar Uncle Rufe use to live. I know
I hain't good fer nothin' much "—he spoke almost huskily; he could scarcely get the words to
his lips—" but I want ye to go with me. Won't
ye?"

The girl did not answer, but her sobbing
ceased slowly, while Rome stroked her hair;
and at last she lifted her face, and for a moment looked to the other shore. Then she rose.
There is a strange pride in the Kentucky mountaineer.

"As you say, Rome, thar's nobody left but
you, 'n' nobody but me; but they burned *you* out,
'n' we hain't even—yit." Her eyes were on
Thunderstruck Knob, where the last sunlight
used to touch the Stetson cabin.

"Hyeh, Rome!" He knew what she meant,
and he kneeled at the pile of kindling-wood near
the kitchen door. Then they stood back and
waited. The sun dipped below a gap in the
mountains, the sky darkened, and the flames rose
to the shingled porch, and leaped into the gathering dusk. On the outer edge of the quivering
light, where it touched the blossomed laurel, the
two stood till the blaze caught the eaves of the
cabin; and then they turned their faces where,

burning to ashes in the west, was another fire, whose light blended in the eyes of each with a light older and more lasting than its own—the light eternal.

THE END

THE LAST STETSON

A MIDSUMMER freshet was running over old Gabe Bunch's water-wheel into the Cumberland. Inside the mill Steve Marcum lay in one dark corner with a slouched hat over his face. The boy Isom was emptying a sack of corn into the hopper. Old Gabe was speaking his mind.

Always the miller had been a man of peace; and there was one time when he thought the old Stetson-Lewallen feud was done. That was when Rome Stetson, the last but one of his name, and Jasper Lewallen, the last but one of his, put their guns down and fought with bare fists on a high ledge above old Gabe's mill one morning at daybreak. The man who was beaten was to leave the mountains; the other was to stay at home and have peace. Steve Marcum, a Stetson, heard the sworn terms and saw the fight. Jasper was fairly whipped; and when Rome let him up he proved treacherous and ran for his gun. Rome ran too, but stumbled and fell. Jasper whirled with his Winchester and was about to kill Rome where he lay, when a

bullet came from somewhere and dropped him
back to the ledge again. Both Steve Marcum
and Rome Stetson said they had not fired the
shot; neither would say who had. Some
thought one man was lying, some thought the
other was, and Jasper's death lay between the
two. State troops came then, under the Governor's order, from the Blue Grass, and Rome
had to drift down the river one night in old
Gabe's canoe and on out of the mountains for
good. Martha Lewallen, who, though Jasper's sister, and the last of the name, loved and
believed Rome, went with him. Marcums and
Braytons who had taken sides in the fight hid in
the bushes around Hazlan, or climbed over into
Virginia. A railroad started up the Cumberland. "Furriners" came in to buy wild lands
and get out timber. Civilization began to press
over the mountains and down on Hazlan, as it
had pressed in on Breathitt, the seat of another
feud, in another county. In Breathitt the feud
was long past, and with good reason old Gabe
thought that it was done in Hazlan.

But that autumn a panic started over from
England. It stopped the railroad far down
the Cumberland; it sent the "furriners" home,
and drove civilization back. Marcums and
Braytons came in from hiding, and drifted one
by one to the old fighting-ground. In time they

took up the old quarrel, and with Steve Marcum and Steve Brayton as leaders, the old Stetson-Lewallen feud went on, though but one soul
was left in the mountains of either name. That
was Isom, a pale little fellow whom Rome had
left in old Gabe's care; and he, though a Stetson
and a half-brother to Rome, was not counted,
because he was only a boy and a foundling, and
because his ways were queer.

There was no open rupture, no organized
division—that might happen no more. The
mischief was individual now, and ambushing
was more common. Certain men were looking
for each other, and it was a question of " drawin' quick 'n' shootin' quick " when the two met
by accident, or of getting the advantage " from
the bresh."

In time Steve Marcum had come face to face
with old Steve Brayton in Hazlan, and the two
Steves, as they were known, drew promptly.
Marcum was in the dust when the smoke cleared
away; and now, after three months in bed, he
was just out again. He had come down to the
mill to see Isom. This was the miller's first
chance for remonstrance, and, as usual, he began to lay it down that every man who had
taken a human life must sooner or later pay for
it with his own. It was an old story to Isom,
and, with a shake of impatience, he turned out

237

the door of the mill, and left old Gabe droning on under his dusty hat to Steve, who, being heavy with " moonshine," dropped asleep.

Outside the sun was warm, the flood was calling from the dam, and the boy's petulance was gone at once. For a moment he stood on the rude platform watching the tide; then he let one bare foot into the water, and, with a shiver of delight, dropped from the boards. In a moment his clothes were on the ground behind a laurel thicket, and his slim white body was flashing like a faun through the reeds and bushes up stream. A hundred yards away the creek made a great loop about a wet thicket of pine and rhododendron, and he turned across the bushy neck. Creeping through the gnarled bodies of rhododendron, he dropped suddenly behind the pine, and lay flat in the black earth. Ten yards through the dusk before him was the half-bent figure of a man letting an old army haversack slip from one shoulder; and Isom watched him hide it with a rifle under a bush, and go noiselessly on towards the road. It was Crump, Eli Crump, who had been a spy for the Lewallens in the old feud and who was spying now for old Steve Brayton. It was the second time Isom had seen him lurking about, and the boy's impulse was to hurry back to the mill. But it was still peace, and without his

238

gun Crump was not dangerous; so Isom rose and ran on, and, splashing into the angry little stream, shot away like a roll of birch bark through the tawny crest of a big wave. He had done the feat a hundred times; he knew every rock and eddy in flood-time, and he floated through them and slipped like an eel into the mill-pond. Old Gabe was waiting for him.

"Whut ye mean, boy," he said, sharply, "reskin' the fever an' ager this way? No wonder folks thinks ye air half crazy. Git inter them clothes now 'n' come in hyeh. You'll ketch yer death o' cold swimmin' this way atter a fresh."

The boy was shivering when he took his seat at the funnel, but he did not mind that; some day he meant to swim over that dam. Steve still lay motionless in the corner near him, and Isom lifted the slouched hat and began tickling his lips with a straw. Steve was beyond the point of tickling, and Isom dropped the hat back and turned to tell the miller what he had seen in the thicket. The dim interior darkened just then, and Crump stood in the door. Old Gabe stared hard at him without a word of welcome, but Crump shuffled to a chair unasked, and sat like a toad astride it, with his knees close up under his arms, and his wizened face in his hands.

Meeting Isom's angry glance, he shifted his own uneasily.

"Seed the new preacher comin' 'long to-day?" he asked. Drawing one dirty finger across his forehead, "Got a long scar 'cross hyeh."

The miller shook his head.

"Well, he's a-comin'. I've been waitin' fer him up the road, but I reckon I got to git 'cross the river purty soon now."

Crump had been living over in Breathitt since the old feud. He had been "convicted" over there by Sherd Raines, a preacher from the Jellico Hills, and he had grown pious. Indeed, he had been trailing after Raines from place to place, and he was following the circuit-rider now to the scene of his own deviltry—Hazlan.

"Reckon you folks don't know I got the cirkit-rider to come over hyeh, do ye?" he went on. "Ef he can't preach! Well, I'd tell a man! He kin jus' draw the heart out'n a holler log! He 'convicted' me fust night, over thar in Breathitt. He come up thar, ye know, to stop the feud, he said; 'n' thar was laughin' from one eend o' Breathitt to t'other; but thar was the whoppinest crowd thar I ever see when he did come. The meetin'-house wasn't big enough to hold 'em, so he goes out on the aidge o' town, 'n' climbs on to a stump. He hed a woman

240

with him from the settlemints—she's a-waitin'
at Hazlan fer him now—'n' she had a cur'us little box, 'n' he put her 'n' the box on a big rock,
'n' started in a callin' 'em his bretherin' 'n' sis-
teren, 'n' folks seed mighty soon thet he meant
it, too. He's always mighty easylike, tell he
gits to the blood-penalty."

At the word, Crump's listeners paid sudden
heed. Old Gabe's knife stopped short in the
heart of the stick he was whittling; the boy
looked sharply up from the running meal into
Crump's face and sat still.

"Well, he jes prayed to the Almighty as
though he was a-talkin' to him face to face, 'n'
then the woman put her hands on that box, 'n'
the sweetes' sound anybody thar ever heerd
come outen it. Then she got to singin'. Hit
wusn't nuthin' anybody thar'd ever heerd; but
some o' the women folks was a snifflin' 'fore she
got through. He pitched right into the feud,
as he calls hit, 'n' the sin o' sheddin' human
blood, I tell ye; 'n' 'twixt him and the soldiers
I reckon thar won't be no more fightin' in
Breathitt. He says, 'n' he always says it mighty
loud "—Crump raised his own voice—" thet
the man as kills his feller-critter hev some day
got ter give up his own blood, sartin 'n' *shore*."

It was old Gabe's pet theory, and he was nod-
ding approval. The boy's parted lips shook

with a spasm of fear, and were as quickly shut tight with suspicion. Steve raised his head as though he too had heard the voice, and looked stupidly about him.

"I tol' him," Crump went on, "thet things was already a-gettin' kind o' frolicsome round hyeh agin; thet the Marcums 'n' Braytons was a-takin' up the ole war, 'n' would be a-plunkin' one 'nother every time they got together, 'n' a-gittin' the whole country in fear 'n' tremblin' —now thet Steve Marcum had come back."

Steve began to scowl and a vixenish smile hovered at Isom's lips.

"He knows mighty well—fer I tol' him— thet thar hain't a wuss man in all these mountains than thet very Steve—" The name ended in a gasp, and the wizened gossip was caught by the throat and tossed, chair and all, into a corner of the mill.

"None o' that, Steve!" called the miller, sternly. "Not hyeh. Don't hurt him now!"

Crump's face stiffened with such terror that Steve broke into a laugh.

"Well, ye air a skeery critter!" he said, contemptuously. "I hain't goin' to hurt him, Uncl' Gabe, but he must be a plumb idgit, a-talkin' 'bout folks to thar face, 'n' him so puny an' spindlin'! You git!"

Crump picked himself up trembling—"Don't

242

ye ever let me see ye on this side o' the river agin, now "—and shuffled out, giving Marcum one look of fear and unearthly hate.

" ' Convicted '! " snorted Steve. " I heerd old Steve Brayton had hired him to waylay me, 'n' I swar I believe hit's so."

" Well, he won't hev to give him more'n a chaw o' tobaccer now," said Gabe. " He'll come purty near doin' hit hisself, I reckon, ef he gits the chance."

" Well, he kin git the chance ef I gits my leetle account settled with ole Steve Brayton fust. 'Pears like that old hog ain't satisfied shootin' me hisself." Stretching his arms with a yawn, Steve winked at Isom and moved to the door. The boy followed him outside.

" We're goin' fer ole Brayton about the dark o' the next moon, boy," he said. " He's sort o' s'picious now, 'n' we'll give him a leetle time to git tame. I'll have a bran'-new Winchester fer ye, Isom. Hit ull be like ole times agin, when Rome was hyeh. Whut's the matter, boy? " he asked, suddenly. Isom looked unresponsive, listless.

" Air ye gittin' sick agin? "

" Well, I hain't feelin' much peert, Steve."

" Take keer o' yourself, boy. Don't git sick *now*. We'll have to watch Eli Crump purty close. I don't know why I hain't killed thet

243

spyin' skunk long ago, 'ceptin' I never had a shore an' sartin reason fer doin' it.

Isom started to speak then and stopped. He would learn more first; and he let Steve go on home unwarned.

The two kept silence after Marcum had gone. Isom turned away from old Gabe, and stretched himself out on the platform. He looked troubled. The miller, too, was worried.

"Jus' a hole in the groun'," he said, half to himself; "that's whut we're all comin' to! 'Pears like we mought help one 'nother to keep out'n hit, 'stid o' holpin' 'em in."

Brown shadows were interlacing out in the mill-pond, where old Gabe's eyes were intent. A current of cool air had started down the creek to the river. A katydid began to chant. Twilight was coming, and the miller rose.

"Hit's a comfort to know *you* won't be mixed up in all this devilment," he said; and then, as though he had found more light in the gloom: "Hit's a comfort to know the new rider air shorely a-preachin' the right doctrine, 'n' I want ye to go hear him. Blood for blood —life fer a life! Your grandad shot ole Tom Lewallen in Hazlan. Ole Jack Lewallen shot him from the bresh. Tom Stetson killed ole Jack; ole Jass killed Tom, 'n' so hit comes down, fer back as I can ricollect. I hev *nuver* knowed hit to fail." The lad had risen on one elbow. His face was pale and uneasy, and he averted it when the miller turned in the door.

" You'd better stay hyeh, son, 'n' finish up the grist. Hit won't take long. Hev ye got victuals fer yer supper ? "

Isom nodded, without looking around, and when old Gabe was gone he rose nervously and dropped helplessly back to the floor.

" 'Pears like old Gabe knows I killed Jass," he breathed, sullenly. 'Pears like all of 'em knows hit, 'n' air jus' a-tormentin' me."

Nobody dreamed that the boy and his old gun had ended that fight on the cliff; and without knowing it, old Gabe kept the lad in constant torture with his talk of the blood-penalty. But Isom got used to it in time, for he had shot to save his brother's life. Steve Marcum treated him thereafter as an equal. Steve's friends, too, changed in manner towards him because Steve had. And now, just when he had reached the point of wondering whether, after all, there might not be one thing that old Gabe did not know, Crump had come along with the miller's story, which he had got from still another, a circuit-rider, who must know the truth. The fact gave him trouble.

" Mebbe hit's goin' to happen when I goes with Steve atter ole Brayton," he mumbled, and

he sat thinking the matter over, until a rattle
and a whir inside the mill told him that the hopper was empty. He arose to fill it, and coming
out again, he heard hoof-beats on the dirt road.
A stranger rode around the rhododendrons and
shouted to him, asking the distance to Hazlan.
He took off his hat when Isom answered, to
wipe the dust and perspiration from his face,
and the boy saw a white scar across his forehead. A little awestricken, the lad walked towards him.

"Air you the new rider whut's goin' to
preach up to Hazlan?" he asked.

Raines smiled at the solemnity of the little
fellow. "Yes," he said, kindly. "Won't you
come up and hear me?"

"Yes, sir," he said, and his lips parted as
though he wanted to say something else, but
Raines did not notice.

"I wished I had axed him," he said, watching the preacher ride away. "Uncle Gabe
knows might' nigh ever'thing, 'n' he says so.
Crump said the rider said so; but Crump might
'a' been lyin'. He 'most al'ays is. I wished I
had axed *him*."

Mechanically the lad walked along the mill-
race, which was made of hewn boards and hollow logs. In every crevice grass hung in thick
bunches to the ground or tipped wiry blades

246

over the running water. Tightening a prop where some silvery jet was getting too large, he lifted the tail-gate a trifle and lay down again on the platform near the old wheel. Out in the mill-pond the water would break now and then into ripples about some unwary moth, and the white belly of a fish would flash from the surface. It was the only sharp accent on the air. The chant of the katydids had become a chorus, and the hush of darkness was settling over the steady flow of water and the low drone of the millstones.

" I hain't afeerd," he kept saying to himself. " I hain't afeerd o' nothin' nor no-*body*; but he lay brooding until his head throbbed, until darkness filled the narrow gorge, and the strip of dark blue up through the trees was pointed with faint stars. He was troubled when he rose, and climbed on Rome's horse and rode homeward—so troubled that he turned finally and started back in a gallop for Hazlan.

It was almost as Crump had said. There was no church in Hazlan, and, as in Breathitt, the people had to follow Raines outside the town, and he preached from the roadside. The rider's Master never had a tabernacle more simple: overhead the stars and a low moon; close about, the trees still and heavy with summer; a pine torch over his head like a yellow plume;

247

two tallow dips hung to a beech on one side,
and flicking to the other the shadows of the people who sat under them. A few Marcums and
Braytons were there, one faction shadowed on
Raines's right, one on his left. Between them
the rider stood straight, and prayed as though
talking with some one among the stars. Behind him the voice of the woman at her tiny or-
gan rose among the leaves. And then he spoke
as he had prayed; and from the first they listened like children, while in their own homely
speech he went on to tell them, just as he would
have told children, a story that some of them
had never heard before. "Forgive your enemies as He had forgiven his," that was his plea.
Marcums and Braytons began to press in from
the darkness on each side, forgetting each other
as the rest of the people forgot them. And
when the story was quite done, Raines stood a
full minute without a word. No one was prepared for what followed. Abruptly his voice
rose sternly—" Thou shalt not kill" ; and then
Satan took shape under the torch. The man
was transformed, swaying half crouched before
them. The long black hair fell across the white
scar, and picture after picture leaped from his
tongue with such vividness that a low wail
started through the audience, and women
sobbed in their bonnets. It was penalty for

bloodshed—not in this world: penalty eternal in the next; and one slight figure under the dips staggered suddenly aside into the darkness.

It was Isom; and no soul possessed of devils was ever more torn than his, when he splashed through Troubled Fork and rode away that night. Half a mile on he tried to keep his eyes on his horse's neck, anywhere except on one high gray rock to which they were raised against his will—the peak under which he had killed young Jasper. There it was staring into the moon, but watching him as he fled through the woods, shuddering at shadows, dodging branches that caught at him as he passed, and on in a run, until he drew rein and slipped from his saddle at the friendly old mill. There was no terror for him there. There every bush was a friend; every beech trunk a sentinel on guard for him in shining armor.

It was the old struggle that he was starting through that night—the old fight of humanity from savage to Christian; and the lad fought it until, with the birth of his wavering soul, the premonitions of the first dawn came on. The patches of moonlight shifted, paling. The beech columns mottled slowly with gray and brown. A ruddy streak was cleaving the east like a slow sword of fire. The chill air began to pulse and the mists to stir. Moisture had gathered on the

249

boy's sleeve. His horse was stamping uneasily, and the lad rose stiffly, his face gray but calm, and started home. At old Gabe's gate he turned in his saddle to look where, under the last sinking star, was once the home of his old enemies. Farther down, under the crest, was old Steve Brayton, alive, and at that moment perhaps asleep.

"Forgive your enemies;" that was the rider's plea. Forgive old Steve, who had mocked him, and had driven Rome from the mountains; who had threatened old Gabe's life, and had shot Steve Marcum almost to death! The lad drew breath quickly, and standing in his stirrups, stretched out his fist, and let it drop, slowly.

II

OLD Gabe was just starting out when Isom
reached the cabin, and the old man thought
the boy had been at the mill all night. Isom
slept through the day, and spoke hardly a word
when the miller came home, though the latter
had much to say of Raines, the two Steves, and
of the trouble possible. He gave some excuse
for not going with old Gabe the next day, and
instead went into the woods alone.

Late in the middle of the afternoon he
reached the mill. Old Gabe sat smoking outside the door, and Isom stretched himself out on
the platform close to the water, shading his eyes
from the rich sunlight with one ragged sleeve.

"Uncl' Gabe," he said, suddenly, "s'posin'
Steve Brayton was to step out'n the bushes thar
some mawnin' 'n' pull down his Winchester on
ye, would ye say, 'Lawd, fergive him, fer he
don't know whut he do'?"

Old Gabe had told him once about a Stetson
and a Lewallen who were heard half a mile
away praying while they fought each other to
death with Winchesters. There was no use

251

"prayin' an' shootin'," the miller declared. There was but one way for them to escape damnation; that was to throw down their guns and make friends. But the miller had forgotten, and his mood that morning was whimsical.

"Well, I mought, Isom," he said, "ef I didn't happen to have a gun handy."

The humor was lost on Isom. His chin was moving up and down, and his face was serious. That was just it. He could forgive Jass—Jass was dead; he could forgive Crump, if he caught him in no devilment; old Brayton even—after Steve's revenge was done. But now— The boy rose, shaking his head.

"Uncl' Gabe," he said with sudden passion, "whut ye reckon Rome's a-doin'?"

The miller looked a little petulant. "Don't ye git tired axin' me thet question, Isom? Rome's a-scratchin' right peert fer a livin', I reckon, fer hisself 'n' Marthy. Yes, 'n' mebbe fer a young 'un too by this time. Ef ye air honin' fer Rome, why don't ye rack out 'n' go to him? Lawd knows I'd hate ter see ye go, but I tol' Rome I'd let ye whenever ye got ready, 'n' so I will."

Isom had no answer, and old Gabe was puzzled. It was always this way. The boy longed for Rome, the miller could see. He spoke of him sometimes with tears, and sometimes he seemed to be on the point of going to him, but he shrank inexplicably when the time for leaving came.

Isom started into the mill now without a word, as usual. Old Gabe noticed that his feet were unsteady, and with quick remorse began to question him.

" Kinder puny, hain't ye, Isom? "

" Well, I hain't feelin' much peert."

" Hit was mighty keerless," old Gabe said, with kindly reproach, " swimmin' the crick atter a fresh."

" Hit wasn't the swimmin'," he protested, dropping weakly at the threshold. " Hit was settin' out 'n the woods. I was in Hazlan t'other night, Uncl' Gabe, to hear the new rider."

The miller looked around with quick interest. " I've been skeered afore by riders a-tellin' 'bout the torments o' hell, but I never heerd nothin' like his tellin' 'bout the Lord. He said the Lord was jes as pore as anybody thar, and lived jes as rough; thet He made fences and barns 'n' ox-yokes 'n' sech like, an' He couldn't write His own name when He started out to save the worl'; an' when he come to the p'int whar His enemies tuk hol' of Him, the rider jes crossed his fingers up over his head 'n' axed us if

253

we didn't know how it hurt to run a splinter
into a feller's hand when he's loggin' or a thorn
into yer foot when ye're goin' barefooted.

"Hit jes made me sick, Uncl' Gabe, hearin'
him tell how they stretched Him out on a cross
o' wood, when He'd come down fer nothin' but
to save 'em, 'n' stuck a spear big as a co'n-knife
into His side, 'n' give Him vinegar, 'n' let Him
hang thar 'n' die, with His own mammy a-standin' down on the groun' a-cryin' 'n' watchin'
Him. Some folks thar never heerd sech afore.
The women was a-rockin', 'n' ole Granny Day
axed right out ef thet tuk place a long time ago;
'n' the rider said, ' Yes, a long time ago, mos'
two thousand years.' Granny was a-cryin',
Uncl' Gabe, 'n' she said, sorter soft, ' Stranger,
let's hope that hit hain't so ' ; 'n' the rider says,
' But hit air so; 'n' He fergive 'em *while they
was doin' it.'* Thet's whut got me, Uncl' Gabe,
'n' when the woman got to singin', somethin'
kinder broke loose hyeh "—Isom passed his
hand over his thin chest—" 'n' I couldn't git
breath. I was mos' afeerd to ride home. I jes
layed at the mill studyin', till I thought my head
would bust. I reckon hit was the Sperit a-workin' me. Looks like I was mos' convicted, Uncl'
Gabe." His voice trembled and he stopped.
" Crump *was* a-lyin'," he cried, suddenly. " But
hit's wuss, Uncl' Gabe; hit's wuss! You say a

life fer a life in *this* worl'; the rider says hit's in
the *next*, 'n' I'm mis'ble, Uncl' Gabe. Ef Rome
—I wish Rome was hyeh," he cried, helplessly.
" I don't know whut to do."

The miller rose and limped within the mill,
and ran one hand through the shifting corn. He
stood in the doorway, looking long and perplex-
edly towards Hazlan; he finally saw, he thought,
just what the lad's trouble was. He could give
him some comfort, and he got his chair and
dragged it out to the door across the platform,
and sat down in silence.

" Isom," he said at last, " the Sperit air
shorely a-workin' ye, 'n' I'm glad of it. But
ye mus'n't worry about the penalty a-fallin' on
Rome. Steve Marcum killed Jass—he can't
fool me—'n' I've told Steve he's got thet penalty to pay ef he gits up this trouble. I'm glad
the Sperit's a-workin' ye, but ye mus'n't worry
'bout Rome."

Isom rose suddenly on one elbow, and with a
moan lay back and crossed his arms over his
face.

Old Gabe turned and left him.

" Git up, Isom." It was the miller's voice
again, an hour later. " You better go home
now. Ride the hoss, boy," he added, kindly.

Isom rose, and old Gabe helped him mount,

255

and stood at the door. The horse started, but the boy pulled him to a standstill again.

"I want to ax ye jes one thing more, Uncl' Gabe," he said, slowly. "S'posin' Steve had a-killed Jass to keep him from killin' Rome, hev he got to be damned fer it jes the same? Hev he got to give up eternal life anyways? Hain't thar no way out'n it—no way?"

There was need for close distinction now and the miller was deliberate.

"Ef Steve shot Jass," he said, "jes to save Rome's life—he had the right to shoot him. Thar hain't no doubt 'bout that. The law says so. But "—there was a judicial pause— "I've heerd Steve say that he hated Jass wuss'n anybody on earth, 'cept old Brayton; 'n' ef he wus glad o' the chance o' killin' him, why—the Lord air merciful, Isom; the Bible air true, 'n' hit says an ' eye fer an eye, a tooth fer a tooth,' 'n' I never knowed hit to fail—but the Lord air merciful. Ef Steve would only jes repent, 'n' ef, 'stid o' fightin' the Lord by takin' human life, he'd fight fer Him by savin' it, I reckon the Lord would fergive him. Fer ef ye lose yer life fer Him, He do say you'll find it agin somewhar— sometime."

Old Gabe did not see the sullen despair that came into the boy's tense face. The subtlety of the answer had taken the old man back to the

256

days when he was magistrate, and his eyes were half closed. Isom rode away without a word. From the dark of the mill old Gabe turned to look after him again.

"I'm afeerd he's a-gittin' feverish agin. Hit looks like he's convicted; but "—he knew the wavering nature of the boy—" I don't know— I don't know."

Going home an hour later, the old man saw several mountaineers climbing the path towards Steve Marcum's cabin; it meant the brewing of mischief; and when he stopped at his own gate, he saw at the bend of the road a figure creep from the bushes on one side into the bushes on the other.

It looked like Crump.

III

IT was Crump, and fifty yards behind him was
Isom, slipping through the brush after him
—Isom's evil spirit—old Gabe, Raines, "con-
viction," blood-penalty, forgotten, all lost in the
passion of a chase which has no parallel when
the game is man.

Straight up the ravine Crump went along a
path which led to Steve Marcum's cabin. There
was a clump of rhododendron at the head of the
ravine, and near Steve's cabin. About this hour
Marcum would be chopping wood for supper,
or sitting out in his porch in easy range from
the thicket. Crump's plan was plain: he was
about his revenge early, and Isom was exultant.

"Oh, no, Eli, you won't git Steve this time.
Oh, naw!"

The bushes were soon so thick that he could
no longer follow Crump by sight, and every
few yards he had to stop to listen, and then
steal on like a mountain-cat towards the leaves
rustling ahead of him. Half-way up the ravine
Crump turned to the right and stopped. Puzzled, Isom pushed so close that the spy, stand-

ing irresolute on the edge of the path, whirled around. The boy sank to his face, and in a moment footsteps started and grew faint; Crump had darted across the path, and was running through the undergrowth up the spur. Isom rose and hurried after him; and when, panting hard, he reached the top, the spy's skulking figure was sliding from Steve's house and towards the Breathitt road; and with a hot, puzzled face, the boy went down after it.

On a little knob just over a sudden turn in the road Crump stopped, and looking sharply about him, laid his gun down. Just in front of him were two rocks, waist-high, with a crevice between them. Drawing a long knife from his pocket, he climbed upon them, and began to cut carefully away the spreading top of a bush that grew on the other side. Isom crawled down towards him like a lizard, from tree to tree. A moment later the spy was filling up the crevice with stones, and Isom knew what he was about; he was making a " blind " to waylay Steve, who, the boy knew, was going to Breathitt by that road the next Sunday. How did Crump know that—how did he know everything? The crevice filled, Crump cut branches and stuck them between the rocks. Then he pushed his rifle through the twigs, and taking aim several times, withdrew it. When he turned away at

last and started down to the road, he looked
back once more, and Isom saw him grinning.
Almost chuckling in answer, the lad slipped
around the knob to the road the other way, and
Crump threw up his gun with a gasp of fright
when a figure rose out of the dusk before him.

" Hol' on, Eli! " said Isom, easily. " Don't
git skeered! Hit's nobody but me. Whar ye
been? "

Crump laughed, so quick was he disarmed of
suspicion. " Jes up the river a piece to see Aunt
Sally Day. She's a fust cousin o' mine by marriage."

Isom's right hand was slipping back as if to
rest on his hip. " D'you say you'd been ' convicted,' Eli? "

Crump's answer was chantlike. " Yes, Lawd!
reckon I have."

" Goin' to stop all o' yer lyin', air ye," Isom
went on, in the same tone, and Crump twitched
as though struck suddenly from behind, " an'
stealin' 'n' *lay-wayin'?* "

" Look a-hyeh, boy—" he began, roughly,
and mumbling a threat, started on.

" Uh, Eli! " Even then the easy voice fooled
him again, and he turned. Isom had a big revolver on a line with his breast. " Drap yer
gun! " he said, tremulously.

Crump tried to laugh, but his guilty face

turned gray. "Take keer, boy," he gasped; "yer gun's cocked. Take keer, I tell ye!"

"Drap it, damn ye!" Isom called in sudden fury, "'n' git clean away from it!" Crump backed, and Isom came forward and stood with one foot on the fallen Winchester.

"I seed ye, Eli. Been makin' a blind fer Steve, hev ye? Goin' to shoot him in the back, too, air ye? You're ketched at last, Eli. You've done a heap o' devilment. You're gittin' wuss all the time. You oughter be dead, 'n' now——"

Crump found voice in a cry of terror and a whine for mercy. The boy looked at him, unable to speak his contempt.

"Git down thar!" he said, finally; and Crump, knowing what was wanted, stretched himself in the road. Isom sat down on a stone, the big pistol across one knee.

"Roll over!" Crump rolled at full length.

"Git up!" Isom laughed wickedly. "Ye don't look purty, Eli." He lifted the pistol and nipped a cake of dirt from the road between Crump's feet. With another cry of fear, the spy began a vigorous dance.

"Hol' on, Eli; I don't want ye to dance. Ye belong to the chu'ch now, 'n' I wouldn't have ye go agin yer religion fer nothin'. Stan' still!" Another bullet and another cut between Crump's 'feet. "'Pears like ye don't think I kin shoot straight. Eli," he went on, reloading the empty chambers, "some folks think I'm a idgit, 'n' I know 'em. Do you think I'm a idgit, Eli?"

"Actin' mighty nateral now." Isom was raising the pistol again. "Oh, Lawdy! Don't shoot, boy—don't shoot!"

"Git down on yer knees! Now I want ye to beg fer mercy thet ye never showed—thet ye wouldn't 'a' showed Steve. . . . Purty good," he said, encouragingly.

"Mebbe ye kin pray a leetle, seein' ez ye air a chu'ch member. Pray fer yer enemies, Eli; Uncl' Gabe says ye must love yer enemies. I know how ye loves me, 'n' I want yer to pray fer me. The Lawd mus' sot a powerful store by a good citizen like you. Ax him to fergive me fer killin' ye."

"Have mercy, O Lawd," prayed Crump, to command—and the prayer was subtle—"on the murderer of this Thy servant. A life fer a life, Thou hev said, O Lawd. Fer killin' me he will foller me, 'n' ef Ye hev not mussy he is boun' fer the lowes' pit o' hell, O Lawd——".

It was Isom's time to wince now, and Crump's pious groan was cut short.

"Shet up!" cried the boy, sharply, and he sat a moment silent. "You've been a-spyin' on us sence I was borned, Eli," he said, reflectively.

262

"Pray fer yer enemies, Eli."

"I believe ye lay-wayed dad. Y'u spied on Rome. Y'u told the soldiers whar he was a-hidin'. Y'u tried to shoot him from the bresh. Y'u found out Steve was goin' to Breathitt on Sunday, 'n' you've jes made a blind to shoot him in the back. I reckon thar's no meanness ye hain't done. Dad's al'ays said ye sot a snare fer a woman once—a woman! Y'u loaded a musket with slugs, 'n' tied a string to the trigger, 'n' stretched hit 'cross the path, 'n' y'u got up on a cliff 'n' whistled to make her slow up jes when she struck the string. I reckon thet's yer wust—but I don't know."

Several times Crump raised his hands in protest while his arraignment was going on; several times he tried to speak, but his lips refused utterance. The boy's voice was getting thicker and thicker, and he was nervously working the cock of the big pistol up and down.

"Git up," he said; and Crump rose with a spring. The lad's tone meant release.

"You hain't wuth the risk. I hain't goin' ter kill ye. I jus' wanted ter banter ye 'n' make ye beg. You're a good beggar, Eli, 'n' a powerful prayer. You'll be a shinin' light in the chu'ch, ef ye gits a chance ter shine long. Fer lemme tell ye, nobody ever ketched ye afore. But you're ketched now, an' I'm goin' to tell Steve. He'll be a-watchin' fer ye, 'n' so 'll I. I tell ye in time,

ef ye ever come over hyeh agin as long as you
live, you'll never git back alive. Turn roun'!
Hev ye got any balls?" he asked, feeling in
Crump's pockets for cartridges. "No; well"
—he picked up the Winchester and pumped the
magazine empty—"I'll keep these," he said,
handing Crump the empty rifle. "Now git
away—an' git away quick!"

Crump's slouching footsteps went out of hearing, and Isom sat where he was. His elbows
dropped to his knees. His face dropped slowly
into his hands, and the nettles of remorse began
to sting. He took the back of one tremulous
hand presently to wipe the perspiration from his
forehead, and he found it burning. A sharp
pain shot through his eyes. He knew what that
meant, and feeling dizzy, he rose and started
a little blindly towards home.

Old Gabe was waiting for him. He did not
answer the old man's querulous inquiry, but
stumbled towards a bed. An hour later, when
the miller was rubbing his forehead, he opened
his eyes, shut them, and began to talk.

"I reckon I hain't much better 'n Eli, Uncl'
Gabe," he said, plaintively. "I've been abusin'
him down thar in the woods. I come might'
nigh killin' him onct." The old man stroked
on, scarcely heeding the boy's words, so much
nonsense would he talk when ill.

" I've been lyin' to ye, Uncl' Gabe, 'n' a-de-
ceivin' of ye right along.   Steve's a-goin' atter
ole Brayton—I'm goin' too—Steve didn't kill
Jass—hit wusn't Steve—hit wusn't Rome—hit
was—" The last word stopped behind his shaking lips; he rose suddenly in bed, looked wildly
into the miller's startled face, and dropping with
a sob to the bed, went sobbing to sleep.

Old Gabe went back to his pipe, and while he
smoked, his figure shrank slowly in his chair.
He went to bed finally, but sleep would not
come, and he rose again and built up the fire and
sat by it, waiting for day.   His own doctrine,
sternly taught for many a year, had come home
to him; and the miller's face when he opened
his door was gray as the breaking light.

IV

THERE was little peace for old Gabe that day at the mill. And when he went home at night he found cause for the thousand premonitions that had haunted him. The lad was gone.

A faint light in the east was heralding the moon when Isom reached Steve Marcum's gate. There were several horses hitched to the fence, several dim forms seated in the porch, and the lad hallooed for Steve, whose shadow shot instantly from the door and came towards him.

"Glad ter see ye, Isom," he called, jubilantly. "I was jus' about to sen' fer ye. How'd ye happen to come up?"

Isom answered in a low voice with the news of Crump's "blind," and Steve laughed and swore in the same breath.

"Come hyeh!" he said, leading the way back; and at the porch he had Isom tell the story again.

"Whut d' I tell ye, boys?" he asked, triumphantly. "Don't believe ye more 'n half believed me."

266

Three more horsemen rode up to the gate and came into the light. Every man was armed, and at Isom's puzzled look, Steve caught the lad by the arm and led him around the chimney-corner. He was in high spirits.

" 'Pears like ole times, Isom. I'm a-goin' fer thet cussed ole Steve Brayton this very night. He's behind Crump. I s'picioned it afore; now I know it for sartain. He's a-goin' to give Eli a mule 'n' a Winchester fer killin' me. We're goin' to s'prise him to-night. He won't be look-in' fer us—-I've fixed that. I wus jus' about to sen' fer ye. I hain't fergot how ye kin handle a gun." Steve laughed significantly. " Ye're a good frien' o' mine, 'n' I'm goin' to show ye thet I'm a frien' o' yourn."

Isom's paleness was unnoticed in the dark. The old throbbing began to beat again at his temple; the old haze started from his eyes.

" Hyeh's yer gun, Isom," he heard Steve say-ing next. The fire was blazing into his face. At the chimney-corner was the bent figure of old Daddy Marcum, and across his lap shone a Win-chester. Steve was pointing at it, his grim face radiant; the old man's toothless mouth was grin-ning, and his sharp black eyes were snapping up at him.

" Hit's yourn, I tell ye," said Steve again. " I aimed jes to lend it to ye, but ye've saved me

267

frum gittin' killed, mebbe, 'n' hit's yourn now—
yourn boy, fer keeps."

Steve was holding the gun out to him now.
The smooth cold touch of the polished barrel
thrilled him. It made everything for an instant clear again, and feeling weak, Isom sat
down on the bed, gripping the treasure in both
trembling hands. On one side of him some one
was repeating Steve's plan of attack. Old
Brayton's cabin was nearly opposite, but they
would go up the river, cross above the mill, and
ride back. The night was cloudy, but they
would have the moonlight now and then for the
climb up the mountain. They would creep close,
and when the moon was hid they would run in
and get old Brayton alive, if possible. Then—
the rest was with Steve.

Across the room he could hear Steve telling
the three new-comers, with an occasional curse,
about Crump's blind, and how he knew that old
Brayton was hiring Crump.

"Old Steve's meaner 'n Eli," he said to himself, and a flame of the old hate surged up from
the fire of temptation in his heart. Steve Marcum was his best friend; Steve had shielded him.
The boy had promised to join him against old
Brayton, and here was the Winchester, brand-
new, to bind his word.

"Git ready, boys; git ready."

THE LAST STETSON

It was Steve's voice, and in Isom's ears the
preacher's voice rang after it. Again that
blinding mist before his eyes, and the boy
brushed at it irritably. He could see the men
buckling cartridge-belts, but he sat still. Two or
three men were going out. Daddy Marcum
was leaning on a chair at the door, looking
eagerly at each man as he passed.

"Hain't ye goin', Isom?"

Somebody was standing before him twirling
a rifle on its butt, a boy near Isom's age. The
whirling gun made him dizzy.

"Stop it!" he cried, angrily. Old Daddy
Marcum was answering the boy's question from
the door.

"Isom goin'?" he piped, proudly. "I
reckon he air. Whar's yer belt, boy? Git
ready. Git ready."

Isom rose then—he could not answer sitting
down—and caught at a bedpost with one hand,
while he fumbled at his throat with the other.

"I *hain't* goin'."

Steve heard at the door, and whirled around.
Daddy Marcum was tottering across the floor,
with one bony hand uplifted.

"You're a coward!" The name stilled every
sound. Isom, with eyes afire, sprang at the old
man to strike, but somebody caught his arm and
forced him back to the bed.

269

" Shet up, dad," said Steve, angrily, looking sharply into Isom's face. " Don't ye see the boy's sick? He needn't go ef he don't want to. Time to start, boys."

The tramp of heavy boots started across the puncheon floor and porch again. Isom could hear Steve's orders outside; the laughs and jeers and curses of the men as they mounted their horses; he heard the cavalcade pass through the gate, the old man's cackling good-by; then the horses' hoofs going down the mountain, and Daddy Marcum's hobbling step on the porch again. He was standing in the middle of the floor, full in the firelight, when the old man reached the threshold—standing in a trance, with a cartridge-belt in his hand.

" Good fer you, Isom! "

The cry was apologetic, and stopped short.

" The critter's fersaken," he quavered, and cowed by the boy's strange look, the old man shrank away from him along the wall. But Isom seemed neither to see nor hear. He caught up his rifle, and, wavering an instant, tossed it with the belt on the bed and ran out the door. The old man followed, dumb with amazement.

" Isom! " he called, getting his wits and his tongue at last. " Hyeh's yer gun! Come back, I tell ye! You've fergot yer gun! Isom! Isom! "

The voice piped shrilly out into the darkness, and piped back without answer.

A steep path, dangerous even by day, ran snakelike from the cabin down to the water's edge. It was called Isom's path after that tragic night. No mountaineer went down it thereafter without a firm faith that only by the direct help of Heaven could the boy, in his flight down through the dark, have reached the river and the other side alive. The path dropped from ledge to ledge, and ran the brink of precipices and chasms. In a dozen places the boy crashed through the undergrowth from one slippery fold to the next below, catching at roots and stones, slipping past death a score of times, and dropping on till a flood of yellow light lashed the gloom before him. Just there the river was most narrow; the nose of a cliff swerved the current sharply across, and on the other side an eddy ran from it up stream. These earthly helps he had, and he needed them.

There had been a rain-storm, and the waves swept him away like thistle-down, and beat back at him as he fought through them and stood choked and panting on the other shore. He did not dare stop to rest. The Marcums, too, had crossed the river up at the ford by this time, and were galloping towards him; and Isom started on and up. When he reached the first bench of the spur the moon was swinging over Thunderstruck Knob. The clouds broke as he climbed; strips of radiant sky showed between the rolling masses, and the mountain above was light and dark in quick succession. He had no breath when he reached the ledge that ran below old Steve's cabin, and flinging one arm above it, he fell through sheer exhaustion. The cabin was dark as the clump of firs behind it; the inmates were unsuspecting; and Steve Marcum and his men were not far below. A rumbling started under him, while he lay there and grew faint—the rumble of a stone knocked from the path by a horse's hoof. Isom tried to halloo, but his voice stopped in a whisper, and he painfully drew himself upon the rock, upright under the bright moon. A quick oath of warning came then—it was Crump's shrill voice in the Brayton cabin—and Isom stumbled forward with both hands thrown up and a gasping cry at his lips. One flash came through a port-hole of the cabin. A yell broke on the night— Crump's cry again—and the boy swayed across the rock, and falling at the brink, dropped with a limp struggle out of sight.

V

THE news of Isom's fate reached the miller by way of Hazlan before the next noon. Several men in the Brayton cabin had recognized the boy in the moonlight. At daybreak they found bloodstains on the ledge and on a narrow shelf a few feet farther down. Isom had slipped from one to the other, they said, and in his last struggle had rolled over into Dead Creek, and had been swept into the Cumberland.

It was Crump who had warned the Braytons. Nobody ever knew how he had learned Steve Marcum's purpose. And old Brayton on his guard and in his own cabin was impregnable. So the Marcums, after a harmless fusillade, had turned back cursing. Mocking shouts followed after them, pistol-shots, even the scraping of a fiddle and shuffling on the ledge. But they kept on, cursing across the river and back to Daddy Marcum, who was standing in the porch, peering for them through the dawn, with a story to tell about Isom.

" The critter was teched in the head," the old

man said, and this was what the Braytons, too, believed. But Steve Marcum, going to search for Isom's body next day, gave old Gabe another theory. He told the miller how Daddy Marcum had called Isom a coward, and Steve said the boy had gone ahead to prove he was no coward.

"He had mighty leetle call to prove it to me. Think o' his takin' ole Brayton all by hisself!" he said, with a look at the yellow, heaving Cumberland. "'N', Lord! think o' his swimmin' that river in the dark!"

Old Gabe asked a question fiercely then and demanded the truth, and Steve told him about the hand-to-hand fight on the mountain-side, about young Jasper's treachery, and how the boy, who was watching the fight, fired just in time to save Rome. It made all plain at last— Rome's and Steve's denials, Isom's dinning on that one theme, and why the boy could not go to Rome and face Martha, with her own blood on his hands. Isom's true motive, too, was plain, and the miller told it brokenly to Steve, who rode away with a low whistle to tell it broadcast, and left the old man rocking his body like a woman.

An hour later he rode back at a gallop to tell old Gabe to search the river bank below the mill. He did not believe Isom dead. It was just his

" feelin'," he said, and one fact, that nobody else thought important — the Brayton canoe was gone.

" Ef he was jus' scamped by a ball," said Steve, " you kin bet he tuk the boat, 'n' he's down thar in the bushes somewhar now waitin' fer dark."

And about dusk, sure enough, old Gabe, wandering hopefully through the thicket below the mill, stumbled over the canoe stranded in the bushes. In the new mud were the tracks of a boy's bare feet leading into the thicket, and the miller made straight for home. When he opened his door he began to shake as if with palsy. A figure was seated on the hearth against the chimney, and the firelight was playing over the face and hair. The lips were parted, and the head hung limply to the breast. The clothes were torn to rags, and one shoulder was bare. Through the upper flesh of it and close to the neck was an ugly burrow clotted with blood. The boy was asleep.

Three nights later, in Hazlan, Sherd Raines told the people of Isom's flight down the mountain, across the river, and up the steep to save his life by losing it. Before he was done, one gray-headed figure pressed from the darkness on one side and stood trembling under the dips. It was

275

old Steve Brayton, who had fired from the cabin at Isom, and dropping his Winchester, he stumbled forward with the butt of his pistol held out to Raines. A Marcum appeared on the other side with the muzzle of his Winchester down. Raines raised both hands then and imperiously called on every man who had a weapon to come forward and give it up. Like children they came, Marcums and Braytons, piling their arms on the rock before him, shaking hands right and left, and sitting together on the mourner's bench.

Old Brayton was humbled thereafter. He wanted to shake hands with Steve Marcum and make friends. But Steve grinned, and said, " Not yit," and went off into the bushes. A few days later he went to Hazlan of his own accord and gave up his gun to Raines. He wouldn't shake hands with old Brayton, he said, nor with any other man who would hire another man to do his " killin'; " but he promised to fight no more, and he kept his word.

A flood followed on New Year's day. Old Gabe's canoe—his second canoe—was gone, and a Marcum and a Brayton worked side by side at the mill hollowing out another. The miller sat at the door whittling.

" 'Pears like folks is havin' bad luck with thar dugouts," said the Brayton. " Some triflin' cuss took old Steve Brayton's jes to cross the river,

276

without the grace to tie it to the bank, let 'lone takin' it back. I've heard ez how Aunt Sally Day's boy Ben, who was a-fishin' that evenin', says ez how he seed Isom's harnt a-floatin' across the river in it, without techin' a paddle."

The Marcum laughed. "Idgits is thick over hyeh," he said. "Ben's a-gittin' wuss sence Isom was killed. Yes, I recollect Gabe hyeh lost a canoe jus' atter a flood more'n a year ago, when Rome Stetson 'n' Marthy Lewallen went a-gallivantin' out'n the mountains together. Hyeh's another flood, 'n' old Gabe's dugout gone agin." The miller raised a covert glance of suspicion from under his hat, but the Marcum was laughing. "Ye oughter put a trace-chain on this un," he added. "A rope gits rotten in the water, 'n' a tide is mighty apt to break it."

Old Gabe said that " mebbe that wus so," but he had no chain to waste; he reckoned a rope was strong enough, and he started home.

"Old Gabe don't seem to keer much now 'bout Isom," said the Brayton. "Folks say he tuk on so awful at fust that hit looked like he wus goin' crazy. He's gittin' downright peert again. Hello!"

Bud Vickers was carrying a piece of news down to Hazlan, and he pulled up his horse to deliver it. Aunt Sally Day's dog had been seen playing in the Breathitt road with the frame of a

human foot. Some boys had found not far
away, behind a withered "blind," a heap of rags
and bones. Eli Crump had not been seen in
Hazlan since the night of the Marcum raid.

"Well, ef hit was Eli," said the Brayton,
waggishly, "we're all goin' to be saved. Eli's
case 'll come fust, an' ef thar's only one Jedg-
ment Day, the Lord 'll nuver git to us."

The three chuckled, while old Gabe sat dream-
ing at his gate. The boy had lain quiet during
the weeks of his getting well, absorbed in one
aim—to keep hidden until he was strong enough
to get to Rome. On the last night the miller
had raised one of the old hearth-stones and had
given him the hire of many years. At daybreak
the lad drifted away. Now old Gabe was following him down the river and on to the dim
mountain line, where the boy's figure was plain
for a moment against the sky, and then was lost.

The clouds in the west had turned gray and
the crescent had broken the gloom of the woods
into shadows when the miller rose. One star
was coming over Black Mountain from the east.
It was the Star of Bethlehem to old Gabe; and,
starlike on both sides of the Cumberland, answering fires from cabin hearths were giving
back its message at last.

"Thar hain't nothin' to hender Rome 'n'
Marthy now. I nuver knowed anybody to stay

'way from these mount'ins ef he could git back;
'n' Isom said he'd fetch 'em.   Thar hain't nothin' to hender—nothin' now."

On the stoop of the cabin the miller turned to
look again, and then on the last Stetson the door
was closed.

THE END

www.ingramcontent.com/pod-product-compliance
Lightning Source LLC
Chambersburg PA
CBHW030956260626
47169CB00002B/570